kill
you
last

kill you last

TODD STRASSER

EGMONT
USA
NEW YORK

EGMONT

We bring stories to life

First published by Egmont USA, 2011
443 Park Avenue South, Suite 806
New York, NY 10016

Copyright © Todd Strasser, 2011
All Rights Reserved

1 3 5 7 9 8 6 4 2

www.egmontusa.com
www.toddstrasser.com

Library of Congress Cataloging-in-Publication Data is available.
LCCN number: 2011936279
ISBN 978-1-60684-024-5
eBook ISBN 978-1-60684-318-5

Book design by Greg Stadnyk

Printed in the United States of America

CPSIA tracking label information:
Printed in September 2011 at Berryville Graphics, Berryville Virginia

To Richie,
who's been there for 43 years.
Thanks, man.

kill
you
last

A TEXT SHOWED UP . . . from Gabriel: **Thx 4 inviting me 2 the party. W2 meet again? 121?**

That caught me by surprise. I could only assume that the quick kiss I'd given him after the party had smoothed out the earlier rough spots. It was flattering to think that he still liked me, but then I thought about the warnings both Whit and Roman had given me about him. I was thinking about how to answer his text when an e-mail popped up: **I like you, Shelby Sloan. If I have to kill you, I'll kill you last.**

chapter 1

"THIS IS AMAZING," Roman said, staring at her iPad. We were sitting at a table in the library, waiting for school to end.

"What now?" I asked.

"*In Cold Blood*, by Truman Capote?" Roman said. "It's one of the best true crime stories I've ever read."

"Coming from you, that's saying a lot."

"And it was written in the *nineteen sixties*," she stressed.

"Oh, you mean, like before the invention of the modern alphabet?"

Roman gave me a droll "You're so funny, Shels."

My BlackBerry vibrated, and I slid it into my lap to read. It was an e-mail, which was odd, since none of my friends ever e-mailed anyone. Stranger still, it was from someone calling themselves vengeance13773288@gmail.com. *This is weird*, I thought, then opened the e-mail:

Ur such a sweet nice girl with Ur perfect house and riding around in daddys Ferrari. 2 bad U dont no what hes really up 2

Roman hooked her black hair behind her ear and looked at me curiously. She must have seen the perplexed expression on my face. "What is it?"

I handed the BlackBerry to her under the table.

"Creep show," she said, handing it back. "Who sends e-mails? And what does he mean by what your dad's really up to?"

"How do you know it's a *he*?" I asked.

"The 'sweet nice girl' part. A girl wouldn't write that." Roman was my best friend and really smart, but sometimes the stuff that came out of her mouth was off-the-charts bizarre.

"Why not?"

"She just wouldn't."

"That makes no sense."

"Says you," Roman replied with a dismissive shrug.

"What should I do?" I nodded at the BlackBerry.

"Write back," Roman said.

"And say what? Who are you, and why did you write this? If he wanted me to know who he was, he wouldn't have used this creepy vengeance at gmail address."

"Say that you already know what your dad does and that you're dealing with it, thank you very much."

"Good idea." I thumbed in the message and pressed Send.

Roman looked past me. "Guess who just came in."

I turned to see Chris Clarke, the tall and broad-shouldered all-state tight end with a 3.9 GPA, signing onto a computer. When he saw me, he smiled and waved. I did the same.

"He's interested," Roman whispered.

"I know." Chris and I had been exchanging looks and smiles for the past week.

"You'd be such a perfect couple," Roman whispered. "Has he said anything?"

I shook my head. "So far it's been all smiles and nods."

"Maybe he's waiting for you to make the first move."

Before I could respond, my BlackBerry vibrated again. It was another message from vengeance13773288@gmail.com. I quickly opened it and found one word: **Liar.**

chapter 2

AFTER SCHOOL, I drove to Dad's studio and parked next to his bright red Ferrari. That car, I sometimes joked, was my only serious competition for his affections. I'd just gotten out of my Jeep when two men I'd never seen before came out of the studio's back door. They got into a dark green sedan, with a laptop computer mounted inside, and drove away. It didn't take a rocket surgeon to figure out that they were police.

I let myself in and started down the wood-paneled hallway lined with autographed head shots of famous models and actors. Almost all the photos were autographed to Dad in black Sharpie with personal thanks and salutations. In the kitchenette, Mercedes was making coffee. Petite and pretty, with dark hair and gold hoop earrings, she was Dad's stylist and general modeling agency gofer.

"*Hola*, Mercedes." I stopped in the doorway. "*¿Cómo está* Pedro?"

Pedro was her little boy, and, at the mention of his name,

Mercedes would usually respond with a big smile and a story about his latest achievement or mischievous behavior. But today her brown eyes slid away, and she fingered the gold cross on her neck. "*Está bien, gracias.*" Her English was fairly good, but I liked to practice my Spanish with her. After high school, I planned to travel around Central America for a few months before starting college.

I wondered if Mercedes's lack of enthusiasm had something to do with those detectives. "What did they want?" I asked.

"You should ask your father."

Her solemn mood was unsettling. "Okay," I said. "How do you say, Give Pedro a hug for me?"

Mercedes smiled weakly. "Pedro *dar un abrazo para mí. Gracias*, Miss Shelby."

I continued down the hall to the office where Janet, Dad's modeling agent and office manager, was standing at a file cabinet with her back to me. I didn't want to startle her, so I knocked gently on the doorframe.

Despite my cautious approach, Janet jumped, the stack of files in her arms spilling to the floor, papers and head shots going everywhere. "Ahhh!" she sort of gasped.

"Sorry," I said.

Someone else might have said, "It's not your fault." But Janet stared haplessly at the papers, photos, and files on the floor. Gray roots showed along the part in her brown hair. "Now what am I going to do? How am I ever going to figure out what goes back in which file?"

"I'll help." I knelt down to gather the files.

"No!" She practically barked. "Leave it alone."

"But—"

"I said leave it. *Please*, Shelby?"

You could see that she was in an extra fragile mood today. When I straightened up, she was trembling. The tiniest things could sometimes send her into histrionics, but it usually took more than a few dropped files.

"What a freaking day." She plopped down on the corner of her desk, crossing her arms tightly and looking jittery. Like the floor, the desk was covered with loose papers and photos. You had to wonder why Dad had hired someone so disorganized to be his office manager.

"What's going on?" I asked.

"Two girls are missing. The dicks wanted to know what we knew about them."

"Were they models?" I asked. Dad's studio and agency did photography and got work for the models he represented.

"We did their head shots," Janet said.

"What happened to them?"

She gestured with a shaky hand to the pile of photos and papers on the floor. "They're probably there somewhere."

"Not the head shots," I said. "I meant, what happened to the girls?"

"Their parents reported them missing. They're probably runaways."

Across the hall, the door to the photo studio opened and Gabriel Gressen, ridiculously gorgeous hunk, part-time model, and Dad's photo assistant, came out with a plate of Chinese food. I felt my heart flutter . . . and not because I found beef with broccoli irresistible.

With his dark eyes, wavy black hair, and chiseled looks, Gabriel was nothing short of drop-dead dreamy. Half the reason I stopped by Dad's studio so often was to gaze upon his Greek-god beauty.

He crossed the hall and stepped into the office, holding out the food. "Anyone interested?"

If only he'd been offering himself, I thought.

"I'll take it." Janet reached for the plate and began to eat hungrily with her fingers.

Gabriel glanced at the papers on the floor as if it was nothing unusual, then smiled at me. "Hey."

My insides turning to Jell-O, I calmly replied, "Hi, what's up?"

"Big glamour shoot today."

"Really? Who?"

"General Tso and his friends Moo Shu and Ginger."

"Hardy-har-har." I showed him I got the joke, then pointed across the hall at the photo studio door. "Can I go in?"

"Sure. The prawns won't mind if you see them undressed."

I went into the photo studio, which, not surprisingly, smelled like a Chinese restaurant. Dad was focusing a camera on a brightly lit plate of chow mein. On a table nearby, a dozen other Asian dishes waited their turn in the spotlight.

"This for a food magazine?" I asked.

"Not exactly." Dad fired a few shots. Strobes popped and flashed, leaving spots in my eyes.

"Advertising?"

"Sort of." He repositioned the plate. "A menu. For the Whacky Wok."

The Whacky Wok was a hole-in-the-wall takeout place on a side street in Soundview. A sign over the counter displayed photos of the various menu items along with corresponding numbers. A wisp of sadness swept over me. In the world of commercial photography, shooting menus was about as low as you could go, especially for a man who'd once done $10,000-a-day fashion shoots. More pops and flashes followed, then Dad replaced the chow mein with what looked like cashew chicken.

"What's with the detectives and the missing girls?" I asked.

"You got me." He adjusted a light. "Seems that we did some shots for their books."

"Books" was model-business slang for the portfolios in which models carried their photos.

"Did they say what they think happened to them?"

"Nah, just asked some questions." Again strobes popped and flashed. Dad seemed totally unconcerned. I decided to show him the strange e-mail from vengeance13773288@gmail.com.

"Interesting," Dad said after reading my BlackBerry.

"Any idea what it means?"

He rubbed his hands together, made his eyes bulge, and grinned maniacally. "I could tell you, my dear, but then I'd have to kill you."

"I'm serious, Dad."

"Seriously?" His shoulders sagged. "Not a clue. Probably just someone playing with your head, you know?"

Sounded logical, I thought. But who?

Dad picked up his camera. "Gotta get this done before the food starts to look soggy. Feel free to take home anything I've finished shooting."

"You won't be home for dinner?"

"Looks like I'll be here pretty late."

I accepted the news with resignation. Dad always had a reason to stay away from home. And not just for late nights at the studio, but on weekends, too, when he'd go out of town to shoot weddings and anniversaries.

I put my arms around his neck and hugged him. "Why don't you have dinner with us tonight?"

"Too much to do here," he said, hugging me back. "But I promise we'll do something special on Sunday, okay? Just the two of us?"

I kissed him on the cheek, took the chow mein, and went back out to the hall. There was no sign of Gabriel. In the office, Janet was thumbing through a file cabinet, the contents of the dropped files still scattered all over the floor, and the half-finished plate of beef with broccoli on her desk. I thought of saying good-bye but didn't want to risk startling her again.

As I passed the kitchenette, Gabriel stepped out. I practically wound up in his arms. "Ah!" I laughed nervously and backed away, feeling my face grow hot. "Sorry!"

He smiled calmly, as if women stepped into his arms all the time, which, come to think of it, was probably true. "Nothing to be sorry about. That was nice." His words had a slightly teasing quality. Meanwhile, those dark eyes burrowed in. "You look pretty."

"Thanks," I said, and almost replied, "You look gorgeous."

"Got a boyfriend?" he asked.

"No one special."

"That's surprising."

"Not if you saw what Soundview High has to offer." That wasn't really the case, but I never let the truth get in the way of snappy repartee.

He smiled again. This wasn't the first time I'd felt attraction vibes emanating from him. But something always seemed to hold him back. I suspected it was because he worked for Dad and was worried that if we started dating and things went sour, it might make for an awkward situation.

Which was too bad.

Maybe I'd have to talk Dad into firing him.

Just kidding.

chapter 3

WHEN I GOT home, Mom was sitting in the kitchen doing a crossword puzzle while she watched TV. The scent of chicken and sweet potatoes was in the air, and the table was set for three. I immediately felt bad that we were going to have yet another dinner without Dad. When Mom saw the chow mein covered with aluminum foil, she scowled.

"I stopped at the studio," I explained. "Dad's doing a Chinese menu. He said he wouldn't be home for dinner."

Her forehead creased, and she nodded silently. There didn't seem to be anything more to say. When I was in grade school, she used to ask how school was, but school was always the same, and even though I was a good student, the best thing about every day was when it was over. So I never wanted to talk about it. Meanwhile, as I grew older, I couldn't help noticing that my parents' relationship grew more and more strained, so when I reached the bratty age of twelve, I had the perfect retort. Each time Mom asked how school was, I'd say, "How're things with Dad?"

It didn't take long for Mom to stop asking about school.

The ironic thing was, now that I was eighteen, I sometimes wished she would.

"What a weird day," I said, putting the food in the refrigerator in case I got hungry later.

"Why do you say that?" Mom asked.

I told her about the detectives and the missing girls, and then showed her the anonymous e-mail.

Mom's eyebrows dipped into a V. "Do you have any idea who it could be from?"

I shook my head. "Could be someone just fooling around."

Mom's scowl deepened. "I'd hate to think that this is someone's idea of a joke."

"Kind of sick, right?"

She nodded. I could have let it drop, but the truth was, there was something else bothering me. It had been bothering me for a long time, long before the anonymous e-mail appeared on my phone, and I knew it had to bother Mom, too, but we'd never spoken about it. Now I was hoping that she would bring it up so I wouldn't have to. When she didn't, I took a deep breath. "Mom, the thing is, you know Dad. Sometimes he can be, well, a little inappropriate."

She stiffened, and I knew immediately that she understood what I was referring to. Our eyes met, and then she gazed off into the distance. Just when I thought that she had nothing to say on the matter, she asked, "Is there something . . . you want to tell me?"

I felt relief that she was willing to listen. "Nothing specific.

But I just can't help wondering if that's what the person who wrote that e-mail meant. I mean, the way Dad sometimes looks at my friends, especially when they're wearing something low-cut? And the things he says. You know . . . things that . . . fathers shouldn't say."

Mom was still looking out the window. It had been sunny earlier, but now the day was gray and shadowless. "I don't know," she said. "It could mean anything. Or maybe you're right, and it's just a prank. There's no way to know."

But what she was really saying was, she didn't want to talk about it.

We ate dinner and watched the news. Mom was all about not rocking the little boat our family sailed through life in. And even though we'd been sailing through stormy waters for years, she seemed reluctant to acknowledge it. To me, Dad was an upsetting contradiction. As a father he could be so much fun, always up for a movie or a game or some crazy spontaneous event in the city, and he was a good sounding board, too, always ready to listen to my problems and help me work through them. But then there was that other man, the one who stared a little too long at my friends, who joked lewdly about women with big chests and short skirts. A lot of men may have thought those things, but leave it to Dad to be the one who verbalized them.

When the commercials came on, Mom muted the TV. "I spoke to Beth today. She has to go to Boston in December, and she's trying to see if she can arrange her flights so that she can visit with us for a day."

"That would be great!" I said. Beth was Mom's younger sister, a vagabond ESL teacher who'd lived all over the world and was currently teaching English in Shanghai. She couldn't afford to come home every year, but when she did, she told wonderfully exotic stories of her adventures. Thanks to her, I planned to get a teaching degree and teach abroad after college.

Mom smiled. Then the commercials ended and the news came back on. She turned up the volume, as if needing to fill the emptiness left by Dad.

Later in my room, video chatting with Roman, I talked about almost winding up in Gabriel's arms that day.

She sighed disapprovingly. "What do you see in him? I mean, yes, he's gorgeous, but you know that deep down he's totally shallow."

"Why do you say that?"

"Uh, hello? The Christmas party?" she said. Every Christmas, Dad had a party in the studio. My friends loved to come because he would take pictures of them posing like models. "All Gabriel could talk about was his car and his apartment and how he made so much money gambling and knew all these famous people. He was so full of himself."

"I think he just does that when he's feeling insecure," I said, trying to defend him. "If you'd seen him today, you'd have a different opinion. He was funny and charming and relaxed. And it really did feel like he was attracted to me. I keep wondering if maybe working with my father is what's holding him back. Couldn't that be it?"

"Shouldn't it be the opposite?" Roman asked. "I mean, don't guys always want to marry the boss's daughter?"

"What if he's worried that if he breaks up with the boss's daughter he'll have a problem with the boss?"

Instead of answering the question, Roman said, "What about Chris Clarke? Harvard, Yale, and Princeton all want him. This time next year, you could be sitting in Harvard Stadium watching him play Yale."

"He's interesting, too," I allowed.

"So?"

"So all he ever does is smile and wave. If he's really serious, why doesn't he do something?"

"Maybe he's shy. Maybe he's waiting to see if you're interested."

"I always wave and smile back," I said. "What else am I supposed to do? Accidentally bump into him and drop my books?"

"Oh God, no. That is so middle school. Why can't you just walk up to him and say hi?"

"I guess I could."

"Could?" Roman echoed.

"Okay, okay. I guess I *will*."

"Hmmm." When Roman made that humming sound, she wanted you to believe that she was thinking about what you'd just said. But it was really her way of taking a moment so that when she changed the topic it wouldn't feel abrupt. "Did you show your dad that e-mail?"

"Yes. He didn't think it was any big deal. But things were

weird there anyway." I told her about the detectives and the two missing girls.

"Seriously?" Roman's interest perked up.

"They're probably just runaways."

"Or it could have something to do with those bodies they found on the south shore of Long Island a few years ago."

I'd heard about that case. For a while the police had suspected two serial murderers were at work. "But they were mostly prostitutes."

"And your point is?" Roman asked.

"Why now, after all that time? Doesn't it make more sense that they're just runaways?"

She hummed for a moment. "Okay, ask your dad if they went for their head shots together or came in separately."

"What difference does it make?"

"Because if they went together, maybe they're friends and ran away together, right? But if they went separately, then it could be something else."

"Roman, come on—"

"Oh, please, *please*? This could be really exciting."

"To you."

"Just ask him if they came in together or separately."

"He's at work."

"It's a five-second phone call. Come on, please? I'll be your friend for life."

"You're already my friend for life."

"Then in the next life, too."

I gave in. The truth was, Roman's interest had piqued my

curiosity, too. Since we were video chatting, I picked up my BlackBerry and called Dad, who answered on the second ring. "Hey, hon, what's up?"

I asked him about the girls.

"Why do you want to know?" Dad asked.

"I was telling Roman about it. You know how she's obsessed with true crime stuff."

"What crime?" Dad asked. "They're just missing. And I'm kind of busy right now."

"I know, Dad. Roman just wants to know if they came together or separately, that's all."

"Probably separately," Dad said. "We do a lot of head shots. It's hard to remember."

Meanwhile, Roman had hastily written something down on a piece of paper and was holding it up on the screen: *Names and where from?*

"Do you remember their names? And where they were from?" I asked.

"Shels . . ." Dad sounded impatient. I wondered why he didn't just answer, since that would have been the fastest way to get off the phone.

"The police must have had some idea," I said.

"Yeah, uh, Rebecca, Margaret, maybe from Pennsylvania or Connecticut or New Jersey, something like that. I really have to get off the phone, hon, okay?"

"Sure, Dad."

We hung up and I told Roman what I'd learned.

"You're the best," Roman said. "Love you. Later." She was

gone, probably to search for every crumb of information she could find about missing girls named Rebecca and Margaret. Meanwhile, I still had homework to do, and an outfit to pick out for an interview at Sarah Lawrence College the next morning. But an hour later, Roman was back on video chat. "Go to the Web site of the National Center for Missing and Exploited Children. Select female, Connecticut, and missing within one year."

I did what she said and three thumbnail photos popped up.

"See Peggy D'Angelo from Hartford?" Roman asked.

"Uh-huh."

"Hit view poster."

I did. Peggy D'Angelo was a round-faced girl described as five feet six inches tall and weighing 135 pounds.

"Now do the same thing with Pennsylvania," Roman said. "This one's name is Rebecca Parlin, from Scranton."

Rebecca Parlin had a bony face and thin lips. She was five feet nine inches and weighed 120 pounds.

"So?" I said.

"Both were aspiring models, *and* both went missing after saying they were going to a mall to meet someone."

I went back and took a closer look. Peggy D'Angelo was cute but, at that height and weight, far from model material. Rebecca Parlin was closer to an acceptable model's height and weight. But she was hardly what you'd call a beauty.

"I bet those are the two girls," Roman said.

"All the way from Hartford and Scranton?" I asked. "Aren't they both, like, hundreds of miles away?"

"About a hundred miles . . . Maybe a two-hour drive."

"It doesn't make sense," I said. "Lots of photographers do head shots. Why would they come all the way to Dad's studio?"

"Good question," said Roman.

I WENT TO the interview at Sarah Lawrence the next morning. Even though I imagined myself going to a large university in a college town like Amherst or Ann Arbor, I'd promised Mom I'd consider Sarah Lawrence because I knew she wanted me to stay close to home. The college had a well-respected teacher-training curriculum, and it was one of the few in the United States that offered an exchange program with the University of Havana in Cuba, which sounded exciting.

I got back to school just as lunch began, and as soon as I stepped into the cafeteria, I sensed that something was off. People stared at me, and tables actually got quiet when I passed. When Roman, sitting at our regular table, saw me, her eyes widened.

"What's going on?" I whispered as I sat down.

"You don't know?" she asked, obviously surprised.

I shook my head and felt apprehensive. Based on the looks I'd just gotten, I realized it was not only something I didn't know, but also something I probably didn't *want* to know.

"There are *three* missing girls," Roman said. "And all of them got head shots by your father. It was on the news a couple of hours ago. There's this Web site called Team Hope where the parents of missing kids compare notes and try to help one another. The parents of Peggy D'Angelo and Rebecca Parlin got together there. And when the parents of the third girl heard about the first two, they got in touch, too."

It took a moment to digest. *On the news* . . . my father and three missing girls? The whole cafeteria knew. No wonder they'd stared. Aware that some kids were still gazing in my direction, I looked down at the lunch table, too uncomfortable to meet their eyes. I would have left, but that would probably draw even more attention.

"What else did they say?" I asked.

"Not much. So far the only things that link the girls are the head shots and going to malls at lunch to meet someone. The police are reviewing security videos from the malls." Roman leaned close and spoke in a low voice. "Last night, when we thought it was just two of the missing girls who'd gotten their head shots from your dad . . . I think I could believe that it might have been a coincidence . . ."

"But not three." I finished the sentence for her. "Did they say where the third one was from?"

"Trenton, New Jersey."

My insides began to knot. Three girls from three different states who all went to my father for head shots, and now all three were missing and the police were investigating. It was bad and awful and upsetting in a way that could compare to nothing thus far in my life. And then there was that feeling I'd had last night that Dad hadn't been completely honest with me. "Be right back." I headed for the small outdoor courtyard beside the cafeteria, careful not to look anywhere except straight ahead. I didn't need to see all those eyes watching me. I could feel them, and that was bad enough.

In the courtyard, I dialed Dad's cell. He answered after the first ring. Given the sudden tumult in my life, there wasn't much I felt I could count on, but one thing was his always answering the phone when I called. "I know why you're calling," he said. "I wish I had an explanation for you, Shels, but I don't." He sounded uncharacteristically glum.

"It can't be a coincidence that all three girls got their head shots from you and now they're all missing."

"I agree," he said, and I felt relieved. At least he wasn't being evasive. I waited for a moment, hoping he'd say something more. Maybe offer some possible explanation. Then I remembered my conversation with Roman the night before. "Dad, there's something else I don't understand. I saw the pictures of two of the girls on the Missing and Exploited Children Web site. They really didn't look like modeling material."

Dad was quiet for a moment. "Well, think about it, Shels. Those were probably family photos with crap lighting and all that. Most of the girls I work with don't look like models until they've had their hair and makeup done, not to mention airbrushing afterward."

"But one of them was five six and weighed a hundred and thirty-five pounds," I said.

"Maybe she wanted to be a plus-size model," Dad said. "There are a lot of possibilities."

It didn't sound right, and I felt my insides twist anxiously. Yes, there probably were *lots of possibilities. . . . Including the possibility that once again I wasn't getting the truth.*

chapter 5

I WAITED, HOPING Dad would say something reassuring, something that would make me believe him, but instead he said, "Hey, what about Sarah Lawrence? Wasn't the interview this morning?"

"It was okay," I said. "I still—"

Before I could finish, Dad interrupted. "Hold on a second?" He was gone, then returned. "They need me in the studio, sweetheart. Talk later?"

"Sure." I made no effort to hide my frustration and disappointment. If he didn't have time and wasn't going to be completely honest with me, I almost didn't want to speak to him.

Feeling upset, I headed back into the cafeteria. I'd always felt closer to him than I had to Mom. Closer to him than anyone else, period. My earliest childhood memories were of him tucking me in every night. Sometimes Mom came into my bedroom, but sometimes she didn't. Even back then, I sensed her absenses had something to do with my little brother, who'd died of pneumonia when he was only six weeks old. But I could always count on

Dad being there every night. If I couldn't trust him, who could I trust?

"Uh, excuse me. Hello?" I was passing a table when a voice stopped me. It was Tara Kraus, a loud, aggressive, politically active type. The other girls at the table were sort of emo-punk, with an emphasis on black mascara and piercings.

"How does it feel to have a creep for a father?" Tara asked.

To say I was flabbergasted was an understatement. I was blown away. It was such a nasty, bizarre, and unexpected question that I couldn't even begin to figure out how to answer it. Instead, I went around them and back to my table.

"What was *that* all about?" Roman whispered when I sat down.

I told her what had happened.

"You're shaking," Roman said.

She was right. I hadn't realized it, but I wasn't surprised. Only now, shock and outrage were giving way to the emotional turmoil that always spelled tears. Thank God my back was to those girls.

Getting through the rest of the day at school wasn't easy. There were moments when I felt angry, others when I felt scared. Mostly, I just couldn't wait for the day to end so that I could be alone. Finally, the last bell rang, and I rushed toward freedom.

In the car, I thought about stopping by the studio, but I decided against it. I was too upset by Dad's evasiveness. When I turned onto my street and saw cars and vans parked along the curb, it didn't register. Sometimes people had parties, and caterers came with vans. And there were always workmen around who drove vans, too. It wasn't until I was in front of my house that I realized they weren't caterers or workmen. They were journalists and camera people hunting for a story.

And I was their prey.

ESCAPE WAS IMPOSSIBLE. The media crowded around my Jeep, just barely leaving enough room for me to pull into my driveway. I parked, and they surrounded the car like a swarm of hungry pigeons fighting for bread crumbs. Not that they were banging on the windows. They just pressed close with their cameras and microphones.

For a few moments I sat with the doors locked, frozen with apprehension and disbelief, totally unnerved by the faces staring in at me. It felt like a standoff. They couldn't get in, and I wasn't sure I wanted to get out. But I couldn't stay in my car forever.

I got out and they moved in, shoving microphones at me, blinding me with flashes, and overwhelming me with questions.

"What did your father have to do with those missing girls?"

"Does he know what happened to them?"

"Do *you* know where they are?"

Backed against the Jeep, I was scared and bewildered. After

all the stress of the afternoon at school, it was too much. The whirlwind of emotions was like a cloudburst, and tears began to pour down my cheeks. Some of the reporters sympathetically backed off, but others pressed forward with more questions, as if sensing that my weakness was their opportunity.

"Did you ever see the girls at his studio?"

"Is it true that he promised them modeling jobs?"

Wiping the tears away, I tried to come up with some way to defend Dad, but it was impossible to think clearly. Was I required to answer? Would it be better if I didn't? What if I said the wrong thing?

Then I became aware of a commotion. Someone was pushing his way through the crowd. Reporters were complaining, warning him to back off, but he was taller and bigger than the others and plowed through with an odd combination of apologies and determination. "Excuse me. Sorry, but I'm coming through." He positioned himself in front of me, and I braced for a new barrage of questions.

"You don't have to put up with this," he said.

I looked up into pale green eyes beneath sandy blond hair, wondering if I'd misheard what he'd said. He seemed younger than the others and was broad through the shoulders and chest, like a football player. He might have been handsome were it not for a bumpy and slightly bent nose.

"Do you want to go into your house?" he asked.

Still rubbing tears away, I nodded and felt an arm go around my shoulders as he led me through the crowd, holding his other arm straight out to keep anyone from getting too close.

"Hey! What are you doing?" someone in the crowd complained.

"Let her talk!"

The media people objected loudly, but he ignored them and guided me to the front door, where he stood like a shield while I unlocked it. I twisted around one last time to look at him and say "Thanks" before I let myself inside.

"Feel better," he said.

chapter 7

IT WAS A huge relief to lock the door behind me. Thank God the kitchen was in the back of the house, so I could sit without feeling all those eyes staring in. Mom wasn't home; she was probably out shopping. I had to warn her, but when I called her cell, I got her voice mail. Still shaking, I poured myself a glass of cold water and sipped slowly. A tight, throbbing pain had started to grow along the sides of my head. I have this bad habit of clenching my teeth when I'm tense, and it causes the muscles above my ears to cramp. If I catch it early and make a conscious effort to relax, I can usually make the pain subside. But sometimes I forget.

The countertop TV came into focus. I turned it on, half expecting to see a video of me in my car, but of course it was too soon for that. Instead, the channels were filled with the typical afternoon talk and cooking shows.

Then, even though I was still upset with him, I called Dad.

"Hi, sweetheart," he answered, sounding weary.

I told him about the media outside our house.

"Yeah, there's a bunch of them hanging around here, too," he said. "Feels like we're defending the Alamo."

The line grew quiet. I wasn't sure what to say next.

"Well, at least you're safe," he said.

It felt like he was ready to get off the phone. But I wasn't finished yet. "Have you talked to the others?"

"What others? Other girls?"

"No, Janet, Gabriel, and Mercedes. Maybe they have some ideas."

"I spoke to them. We're all in the dark. Nobody even remembers those girls. We've probably done close to a thousand head shots in the past three years. We looked at the photos the detectives had, and none of us recognized them. I mean, it doesn't make any sense. If the girls had all come from the same town, you might think they got together and ran off to Hollywood or something. But they live so far away from each other. It's crazy."

It felt and sounded like he was being completely honest, and I was relieved. In a way, it was reassuring. No matter what anyone else said, I could tell that he wasn't hiding anything.

"Oh, so let me tell you about our escape plan," Dad said. "We're going to disguise Gabe and let him take the Ferrari. Hopefully, the media will think it's me and follow him."

"Meanwhile, you'll sneak out?" I guessed.

"Right. Janet will give me a ride home."

"You're really going to let Gabriel have the Ferrari?"

"Yeah. He's thrilled. You know how he's always wanted to drive it."

I did. And I also knew how protective Dad was of his car.

Just the idea that he was willing to let someone else use it was a measure of how crazy things had become.

"We're going to wait until it gets dark," Dad said. "Otherwise, someone may notice that it's Gabe in a disguise. So I'll see you at home later, okay, sweetheart?"

"Sure."

He got off the phone, and I speed-dialed Mom again. This time I got her and warned her about the crowd in front of our house. "Maybe you could park in front of the Sisks' house and then cut through the backyards and come in the back door."

Twenty minutes later, Mom came in through the kitchen door and put her shopping bags on the table. "This is unbelievable," she muttered.

"At least you got in without being surrounded," I said.

Mom frowned. She was such a quiet, orderly person; she must've hated the media circus trampling the lawn outside.

"You heard about the third missing girl also being one of Dad's clients?" I asked.

She nodded.

"It's freaky, Mom. What do you think's going on?"

Her eyebrows rose with surprise. "Don't jump to conclusions, Shelby. They're only missing."

"I know, but it's still weird. I talked to Dad before. It really sounds like he doesn't have a clue, either."

Mom glanced away and didn't respond. I wished I could get her to open up and tell me what was on her mind.

"You believe that, don't you?" I asked. "That he doesn't have a clue?"

Mom's forehead wrinkled, and she placed a reassuring hand over mine. "Of course I do. Your father wouldn't hurt a fly. Those girls will probably turn up somewhere in a day or two."

I wanted to believe her, but I knew she was better than most when it came to sticking her head in the sand and avoiding upsetting topics. Sensing that I wouldn't get any further, I changed the subject. "I went to that interview at Sarah Lawrence this morning. It's a nice school."

Mom brightened. "I'm so glad."

"But I still want to visit some bigger campuses. Someplace with a real college town around it."

She pressed her lips together. The smile vanished. "There's no place like that nearby."

"Mom, even if I went to Sarah Lawrence, I'd want to live in a dorm. I wouldn't live at home."

She nodded and looked a little crestfallen. Sometimes I felt like she wanted me to stay home and be her little girl forever. Part of me understood why. Beth once told me that before Mom lost my little brother, she'd been a gregarious, outdoorsy type who loved to go camping and take long hikes. But after he died, she'd retreated to the indoors, becoming overprotective and cautious, at times so introverted that it almost felt like she was living in her own world. Like the way she made a place setting for Dad every night despite the fact that he hardly ever ate dinner with us. How could she pretend that we were a happy family when Dad had moved into the guest bedroom four years ago? He said it was because of his snoring, but I wasn't stupid. There was no affection between them, and they almost never went out together. Was that the reason Mom didn't want me to go far away to college? Because without me, she had nothing?

I went upstairs and got online to tell Roman about being ambushed by the media.

"It's like being famous, but for all the wrong reasons," she said.

"Tell me about it," I grumbled, and then I told her about Dad's plan to sneak out of the studio after dark. "Gabriel's going to take the Ferrari to his place."

"If he doesn't drive all over town first, showing off to his friends," Roman quipped in a snarky tone.

I sensed that she was about to launch into a recitation of all the things she disliked about him, so I quickly changed the subject. "What else is going on? What are they saying at school?"

On the screen, Roman looked down at her keyboard, so all I saw was the part in her hair. When she looked back up, her lips were a flat, straight line. I knew the news wasn't going to be good.

"It's all they're talking about. I was chatting with Sabrina and some girls from the *Bugle*, and they were comparing notes. Like things your father had said to them, or the way they sometimes caught him looking at them. The general feeling is that he's probably responsible for whatever happened to those girls."

I shouldn't have been surprised, but I still felt like I'd been stabbed in the gut. It was so unfair. Why didn't Sabrina come to me in person? We'd been teammates on intramural volleyball for years.

"Mom says they probably ran away and will pop up in a day or two," I said.

"Three girls from different states ran away together?" Roman repeated dubiously.

I winced at how dumb that must've sounded. On the screen, Roman's eyebrows dipped with concern. "Should I not be saying this stuff?"

"No, it's okay. . . . I guess."

"If you ask me, it's just plain sucky," Roman said. "I mean, I like your dad, and I think it's a ridiculous leap from catching someone staring at your cleavage to assuming he's going around hurting people, but—"

"Wait," I said. "Nobody said anyone's been hurt. Maybe they didn't run away *together*, but that doesn't mean they didn't go somewhere. They could have all joined a cult."

"The Kirby Sloan head shot cult?"

I sighed. "Let's talk about something else." I told her about my interview at Sarah Lawrence that morning, and Roman told me that she'd decided to apply early decision to Skidmore, where she wanted to pursue art and dance. When we finished, I closed my laptop and sat on my bed, feeling really, really down about the rumors concerning Dad. Was it partly my fault for never saying anything to him about the way he sometimes acted around my friends? I guess there are parts of our lives that we're aware of, but we try to make them go away by not thinking about them. I realized I was guilty of the same thing Mom was—we believe that if we don't think about certain problems, they won't be true. There'd been so many embarrassing things Dad had said over the years. . . . Like once he'd asked me what Courtney's bra size was. And then there was the time he wanted to know what my friends and I talked about when we took showers after gym, and other times when he made sexist jokes that I found seriously distasteful. And then there was the Ferrari, and how before I was old enough to drive, he used to love to pick me up at school in it. Nothing seemed to make him happier than when one of my friends asked if he would take her for a ride around the block before we went home. And since it was a two-seater, that always meant going off with her alone.

If only I'd said something, told him that some of the things he did and said were borderline creepy . . . Maybe it would have made a difference. Maybe he would have been more careful about the way he acted and we wouldn't be in this situation now, where everyone assumed he was guilty of having something to do with those missing girls.

But like everything, there was another side to the story. Most of the fun times I'd had with my family had come because Dad had gotten us to go out and do something. And when I was upset, he'd always been the one I'd gone to, the one I could depend on to help me feel better. Mom never seemed to understand me the way he did, and for that reason I needed him and was a little afraid of doing anything that might make him angry. So as those moments came when maybe I should have said something about his behavior, I'd just tried to laugh it all off, saying things like "Oh, it's just Dad being Dad" and "He's harmless." Because, I realized now, that's what I wanted to believe.

My BlackBerry buzzed. I picked it up and felt my jaw tighten.

It was another e-mail from vengeance13773288@gmail.com:
Wre I 2 die today, my dying wish would B 2 C Ur dad get what he deserves.

I sat up on the side of my bed, thinking I should show it to Mom, but then caught myself. She was already upset about what was happening with Dad and with imagining a life without me at home. Showing her another e-mail like this wouldn't help. The best thing I could do about this latest e-mail, I decided, was to keep it to myself.

And there was something else: like the last one, this message had come as an e-mail, but was written like a text. What did that say about the person who'd sent it?

chapter 8

I'D GIVEN UP on my homework and was skipping around the Internet, looking for news updates, when Dad knocked on my door and came in. The lines in his face looked deeper than usual, and his eyes were ringed.

"How's it going?" he asked, trying to sound jocular.

"Not very good, but probably better than it's going for you."

He plopped down wearily on the edge of my bed. "I'm sorry about all this, sweetheart. Really can't make heads nor tails of it. But it's good that the police are involved. Sooner or later they'll figure out what's going on with those girls. And then we'll be able to get back to normal."

It was a relief to hear him say that. Surely someone guilty of wrongdoing wouldn't be so welcoming of police involvement.

"I ask a favor?" he said. "We pulled off our little masquerade, and Gabe's bringing the Ferrari over. Someone has to drive him back home."

I felt my heart leap unexpectedly. "Oh, uh, sure, Dad, I can do that," I said, as if it was the right thing for a daughter to do. But the truth was, despite everything that was going on, I couldn't help but feel excited by the thought of being alone in a car with Gabriel.

"Thanks, sweetheart." Dad managed a weak smile. "And don't worry. We'll get through this."

As soon as he left my room, I started to look through my closet for something to wear. I did feel a little guilty about trying to look nice during a family crisis, but I couldn't help it. I wanted to look my best for Gabriel. I was in the bathroom doing my makeup when I heard the high-pitched whine of the Ferrari's engine outside.

Dad called up the stairs. "Shels? Time to go."

Downstairs, Gabriel was in the hall with Dad. I know it was only my imagination, but I wanted to believe that they were both captivated as I came down the steps like a movie star descending a curved marble staircase. My fantasy was brief. Thinking more about the car than about me, Gabriel turned to Dad and said, "Can't I drive it back to my place and then Shelby can drive it home?"

"You've had enough fun for one day," Dad replied.

Gabriel tossed him the key fob with the famous prancing black horse. A few minutes later we drove out of the driveway in my Jeep. The few journalists still hanging around outside looked up as we passed, but no one showed much interest. Meanwhile, I nervously racked my brain for something clever to say. Luckily, Gabriel had a question.

"Does he ever let you drive it?"

"The Ferrari? Just once."

"Why? Something happen?"

"I backed it out of the driveway, and he said I didn't come to a complete stop before I shifted into first."

"So you know how to drive a stick?" Gabriel sounded impressed.

"Before the Ferrari, we had a Porsche. That's what I learned on. Dad taught me to drive in a parking lot when I was fourteen. He thinks it's sexy when a woman can drive a stick." But now I wondered, had it been appropriate for Dad to say to me, his daughter, that driving a stick was sexy?

"I'd have to agree," Gabriel said.

I sensed an opportunity to flirt, but given the circumstances, it felt wrong. Instead, I changed the subject. "So what do you think's going on?"

"Who knows? It's crazy."

"In what way?"

"In *every* way."

"Like all three missing girls getting head shots from Dad?"

"Yeah, and . . ." For a second it seemed like he was going to add something more.

"And?" I prompted him to continue.

"And just, you know, the whole thing. The cops questioned everyone at the studio, but you could see they were more interested in your father and me because we're guys. As if we might have had a reason to go around doing evil things to women."

I wanted to ask him more, but before I could, he reached over and flicked away some strands of hair that had fallen into my face.

When his fingers brushed my cheek, I felt a shivery tingle.

"That's better," he said. "Anyone ever tell you that you have a beautiful profile?"

The tingling increased. I'd been told I had a nice profile, but I couldn't recall anyone saying it was beautiful. That felt good, especially from someone like Gabriel, who had certainly spent a lot of time around beautiful women.

"Uh, no," I answered. "But thanks."

"I wonder . . ." He reached behind me and gathered my hair in his hand as if putting it in a ponytail. I felt goose bumps as his fingers grazed the nape of my neck. "How come I never see you in a ponytail?"

Was he indicating that he paid more attention to me than I'd previously thought? How else would he know that I almost never put my hair in a ponytail?

"Only when I'm playing sports," I said.

"Which ones?"

"Tennis, snowboarding, volleyball. I used to play soccer."

"We should go boarding sometime," he said, then pointed through the windshield. "That's it, on the right." The building was new and brightly lit, with a canopy stretching out to the street. As I slowed down, a doorman stepped out.

Gabriel turned to me. "Thanks for the ride."

"You're welcome." I smiled.

The doorman opened the passenger door. Gabriel started to get out, then stopped and turned back to me. "Feel like a quick drink?"

chapter 9

MY FIRST IMPULSE was to say yes, but I quickly caught myself. Just suppose the girls hadn't run away? Suppose something bad *had* happened to them. Anyone associated with the studio had to be a possible suspect, right? And besides Dad, Gabriel was the only other male who worked there.

But the chances were slim that something bad had happened. Like Mom said, in a day or two it would probably all be cleared up.

And I did have a crush on Gabriel, who hardly seemed like a violent, girl-abductor type. With looks like his, he was probably more concerned with being abducted himself.

Those girls could have all run off and joined the circus.

I was dying to see Gabriel's apartment.

And Dad knew where I was.

"Okay, sure," I heard myself say.

We rode up in an elevator lined with mirrors. Gabriel smiled, and I smiled back nervously, then noticed that his gaze went past me to his reflection in the mirrored elevator wall. I was surprised since, in my estimation, he was the last man on earth who needed to be concerned about his appearance.

A few moments later, while I stood in the hall, waiting for him to unlock the door, I realized that I'd never been in a single man's apartment before. The door opened into darkness, and I began to feel apprehensive. *Was this a smart thing to do?* Gabriel turned on a light, and I felt my jaw drop. He may have been only a few years older than me, but his apartment was gorgeous, spacious, with art on the walls and a granite counter separating the kitchen from the living room. There were black leather couches; thick rugs; tall, elegant lamps; and sheer curtains. I couldn't help wondering if he'd done it all himself or hired a decorator, and where he'd gotten all the money. Definitely not from being an assistant at Dad's studio while picking up a few local modeling jobs here and there.

"Welcome to the apartment Texas hold 'em built," he said, as if he knew what I was thinking.

"That's a card game, right?"

"Not *a* card game," he said. "*The* card game. Played in casinos around the world." He went around the granite counter. "Vino?"

I wasn't a big fan of wine, especially on an empty stomach, which was the result of my having no appetite after all the anxiety from earlier in the day. But asking for a soft drink sounded way too middle school. So I said yes.

"Perfecto." Gabriel placed two wineglasses on the counter, then took a bottle from the refrigerator. "I've got a really smooth Chardonnay."

I sat on a stool feeling tense, but excited. This was all so very mature, and more than a little nerve-racking. He handed me a glass. "Cheers."

I imagined tapping my glass too hard against his, and both shattering in a burst of shimmering liquid and shards. Plus, given the circumstances, I wasn't sure what there was to toast. But I managed to clink glasses and then take just enough of a sip to reconfirm the fact that I really didn't like the taste.

Gabriel put down his glass and gazed past me at the dark windows. I glanced in the same direction and realized he was looking at his reflection again. Was it nervousness or, as I was beginning to suspect, something more narcissistic?

He gestured toward the living room. "Shall we sit someplace more comfortable?"

I would have preferred keeping the kitchen counter between us, but again, I couldn't imagine how to say no to his offer. The couch was L-shaped and I sat down close to the vortex, hoping he'd sit opposite me. Instead, he came around the coffee table and sat beside me. I felt my jaw tighten and a headache looming. Despite all the times I'd fantasized about being with him, this was definitely a be-careful-what-you-wish-for moment.

"How do you like it?" he asked, taking another sip of wine.

"Uh, very good." I took a sip and thought, *Yuck.*

"Well balanced, right? Not too sweet and fruity."

"Right."

Gabriel placed his glass on the coffee table and turned to me. "So, Shelby Sloan . . ."

I knew what that look, and tone of voice, meant. Maybe, at some other time and under other circumstances, I might have welcomed it, but given the reason I'd had to drive him home tonight, it seemed strange and out of place.

"I can't get my mind off what's going on," I said.

Gabriel's face fell and he sighed, then took another sip of wine and leaned toward me until our shoulders touched. "I know you're worried about your dad. But I wouldn't make too much of it. He's really good at dealing with stuff. Believe me, I've seen him in action. Whatever this is about, it'll blow over, and we'll get right back to business."

He meant to reassure me, but his words struck me as weird and jarring. You might have thought he was talking about something as insignificant as a traffic ticket or a hacked Facebook account, not three missing human beings. I began to think back to what Roman had said about Gabriel's being shallow. Maybe she was right. Maybe Chris Clarke would be a better fit for me. Meanwhile, the pressure of his shoulder on mine increased as he leaned closer. "I still find it hard to believe that someone as attractive as you doesn't have a boyfriend."

"Not at the moment," I blurted out, then immediately wished I hadn't. I didn't want to sound like I was implying that he could fill the position. Right?

Or did I?

I closed my eyes and was surprised to feel things begin to wobble. That's when I knew it was time to go. This was the wrong time to be here. It wasn't Gabriel's fault. Not after all the hints I'd dropped around the studio. The worst he could be accused of was being a little callous about the missing girls. But I wasn't sure that was any worse than what I'd done by agreeing to come up to his place and have a glass of wine.

"I have to go," I said, and got up.

"You sure?" Gabriel asked, surprised.

"There's school tomorrow, and I still have some homework to do. But thanks for the drink and for showing me your place. It's really beautiful." I walked so quickly toward the door that Gabriel practically had to jog to keep up. So much for trying not to act like I was in middle school.

He got to the door at the same time I did. I assumed he was just being a gentleman and opening it for me.

But instead, he put his hand on the doorknob and kept it there.

I felt myself go rigid.

Was he going to stop me from leaving?

He moved close, and I felt a shiver.

"Gabriel, please, not now," I heard myself say, trying very hard not to sound scared or panicked.

I felt his finger go under my chin and gently lift it until our eyes met.

"Another time, then?"

"Yes," I said, silently begging him to let go of the door.

He turned the doorknob and at the same time kissed me on the lips. It was just a peck, and it happened much too fast for me to react. The door swung open, and the next thing I knew, I was striding down the hall to the elevator.

I pressed the button and waited, my heart thumping. Out of the corner of my eye, I saw Gabriel standing in his doorway, watching.

As the elevators opened, he said, "Hey."

I turned, and he gave me a smile and a wave. "Get home safe."

I drove home super careful. Not that I'd had that much to drink, but I was rattled. What had just happened? The more I thought about it, the more uncertain I was about what bothered me so much.

Was it the way Gabriel had acted?

Or the way I had?

What was the big deal? It was just a drink in his apartment. He really hadn't made any unwanted moves, and even if he had, so what? I'd had plenty of experience dealing with that.

So then, what *was* it that bothered me so much? I didn't really know. Maybe something intuitive. Or maybe just my imagination.

By the time I got back to my neighborhood, I felt calmer. I'd decided that neither of us was at fault. We'd just gotten our signals crossed.

I parked in the driveway. By now the media was gone, and only a few dark cars were parked on the street in front of our house. I got out, pausing for a moment to breathe in the fresh cool air and gaze up at the stars sparkling in the sky.

That's when I realized someone was coming up the driveway toward me.

It was a man.

And he was big.

chapter 10

MY GASP OF fright must have been loud, because he suddenly stopped. By then I'd backed partway around the car and was on the verge of letting out the loudest scream I could muster.

We stared at each other, and in the dark I recognized him as the one who'd helped me through the crowd of media people and into my house earlier in the day.

"What do you want?" I asked in a quavering voice, my heart racing like a hamster full tilt on a wheel.

"Sorry," he apologized. "Didn't mean to scare you. I just wanted to catch you before you went inside."

"Oh." I was still breathing hard. "Okay, but from now on? It's really not a good idea to approach people in the dark like that."

"Gotcha. Like I said, I'm sorry. You okay?"

"Just a little freaked," I said. "So what are you doing here?"

"I was hoping I could ask you some questions."

"Questions?"

"About those missing girls?"

"Why?" I was still too flustered to follow.

"I'm a journalist."

Suddenly, I got it. "So that's why you helped me into the house today? To get me away from all those other journalists so that later on, you could find me alone and get the story for yourself? Smart. I'm impressed. You'll go far." I came around the car and started toward the back door, feeling incensed and angry. The one thing you could always count on when guys were nice was that they usually wanted something.

"Wait," he said.

"Sorry. I've had a really long, hard day." I kept walking. "So just please go away."

"But—"

"Are you aware that you're trespassing?" I asked as I opened the back door. "If you don't get off my property right now, I'm calling the police."

"What did you think of Sarah Lawrence?" he asked.

Halfway in the door I stopped and stared through the dark at him, confused. "How . . . ?"

"We passed each other this morning," he said. "At school. I mean, my school, not yours."

"You go to Sarah Lawrence?"

"Go, black squirrels," he said.

I'd noticed that morning that black squirrels were some sort of informal Sarah Lawrence mascot, which had seemed strange, though not as strange as the idea that this guy had actually seen me there.

"Yeah, I meant to ask someone about that," I said, feeling myself relax. "What's the story?"

"The black squirrels?" he asked. "They used to be the unofficial school symbol, but now the administration wants us to think of ourselves as mighty gryphons, the mythical half lion/half eagle." He held out his hand. "I'm Whit."

I hesitated, then decided it couldn't hurt to shake. My hand disappeared in his. "I'm Shelby. I've never met a Whit before."

"Short for Whitman. Whitman Sturges. That's how you know I'm a WASP. Both of my names could be either first or last. Whitman Sturges, or Sturges Whitman."

Strangely, that made me smile. Maybe after such a hellish day, what I really needed was a little levity. "So you're a WASP gryphon black squirrel?

"You got it. I can fly. I can sting. I've got sharp teeth. And I know where all the nuts are buried."

I grinned. "We really passed each other at Sarah Lawrence this morning?"

"You were taking the campus tour. And then later I drove over here to cover the story, and there you were again. What my statistics professor would call an infinitely improbable coincidence."

There was something about him that put me at ease. That disarming quality some people have that makes you believe whatever they're saying. I wondered if he'd developed it to compensate for his intimidating size and presence.

"But you're also a reporter?" I asked.

"A stringer. For the *Snoop*."

"The what?"

"The *Soundview Snoop*? Your up-to-the-minute hyper-local news site? www.soundsnoop.com."

"Never heard of it," I said.

His broad shoulders sagged with disappointment. "Tell me about it. Neither has anyone else. It's still pretty new. And the only place on the Net where you can find out which of your neighbors broke the pooper-scooper law last week."

"So it's online?"

"Electronic journalism is the future. Newspapers are the past. Pretty soon we'll have so many trees, we won't know what to do with them."

Once again I found myself smiling. "So why did you say you're a stringer? I thought that's what people did to tennis rackets."

"It's an old newspaper term. Basically means I'm a freelancer. Only when you're freelancing for an Internet start-up, the emphasis is on *free*."

"Aren't you keeping pretty long hours, considering you're not getting paid?"

"I look at it as learning on the job. Like an internship. And who knows? If I do well on this story . . . maybe even scoop some of the professional journalists . . . some news organization might be crazy enough to hire me for real."

Suddenly, I felt as if I'd awoken from a spell. As if, for just a moment, I'd forgotten what a journalist did. Why was I talking to him? All his charming banter served one purpose—to get a story about my father.

"You are good, you know that?" I said, feeling my jaw tighten. "You almost had me. But I get it now. All this is to you is a chance to get a story. Meanwhile, my father's reputation . . . my family's whole life . . . is on the line. And there hasn't been a single shred of evidence connecting him to those missing girls except some head shots. . . . God, I can't believe I even spoke to you. You don't even go to Sarah Lawrence, do you? This isn't an indisputably unlikely coincidence, or whatever you called it. You probably followed me this morning and made this whole thing up just to get me to drop my guard. I'm counting to three, and if you're not off my property, I'm calling nine-one-one."

"But—" he began.

I got out my BlackBerry. "One . . . two . . ."

He raised his hands. "Okay, okay, you win." He turned and headed back down the driveway. But as I let myself into the house, I heard him call, "I really do go to Sarah Lawrence."

Still annoyed with myself for coming so close to being suckered, I went inside and locked the door. The kitchen was dark, and I pressed my back to the door, trying to calm down. Then I became aware of voices coming from the living room.

"What exactly did you think was going to happen?" Mom asked, sounding angry and upset.

"I know, I know," Dad answered, with a subdued, regretful voice. "I didn't think."

"No kidding," Mom practically spat. Her tone caught me by surprise. I wasn't sure I'd ever heard her be so harsh.

"So what do I do?" Dad asked.

"You tell the truth. Those girls came to you for head shots, and yes, it looks very suspicious now that they're missing, but you have absolutely no idea what happened to them. That *is* the truth, isn't it?"

"Yes."

"You're *sure?*" Mom pressed.

"*I said yes, Ruth.*" Dad's answer was more emphatic.

"Then I don't understand what your problem is," Mom said.

There was silence for a moment. Then Dad said, "Should I hire a lawyer?"

In the quiet that followed, I wondered why he'd ask that if he was innocent.

As if she'd read my thoughts, Mom said, "If you hire a lawyer, people will instantly begin to wonder why you feel you need one."

"But if I don't, I feel totally vulnerable. What if I say the wrong thing? I feel like it's me against the whole world."

I felt a pang when I heard that. My parents had been married for twenty years, and now Dad was basically saying that he didn't feel like he could count on Mom for emotional support. I felt the urge to go down the hall and tell him that he'd always have my support. But I knew better than to get between them. I could tell him later.

I waited for Mom's answer, hoping that she'd reassure him that he wasn't all alone, that she'd stand by him. But it was Dad's voice I heard next. "I guess, at this point, Ruth, saying I'm sorry doesn't mean very much."

Again there was silence. What was Dad saying he was sorry for? For the iciness that had grown between them? For choosing to sleep in a separate bedroom? I still didn't know what had caused all their ill will in the first place. Was that what he was talking about?

chapter 11

I GOT INTO bed with my laptop and looked for news, but there'd been no new developments during the day. The police were still "looking into the situation." I took a look at the *Snoop*, too, which featured mostly Soundview-centric information about town government, schools, and complaints about leaf-blower noise. But I purposefully stayed off video chat and IMs.

Later I lay in the dark with unanswered questions instead of dreams. If Dad had no connection to the three missing girls, why was he thinking about hiring a lawyer? Who was vengeance13773288@gmail.com, and what did he know about this? And what had Dad apologized to Mom for, knowing ahead of time that she wouldn't accept his apology?

I woke with a jolt, the alarm like a buzz saw five inches from my ear. I felt like I'd hardly slept at all, but sunlight filtered in through the shades. Fumbling to turn off the alarm, I accidentally knocked it to the floor, where it continued to buzz out of reach. Burying my head under the pillows didn't work, so finally I dragged my sleep-deprived body out of bed. But even before I hit the shower, I checked the computer. Roman was on. Sometimes I wondered if she ever slept.

"S'up?" I asked with a yawn.

"Have you seen what's on TV this morning?" she asked.

Despite the cobwebs in my brain, I knew her question meant bad news. "Oh God, now what?"

On the screen, I watched as Roman aimed her webcam at the small TV on her desk. A teenage girl was being interviewed by a news anchor in a studio. In the top right corner of the screen was a small box with a photo. It took a moment for me to realize it was Dad.

"So how did this scam, as you call it, work?" the blonde anchorwoman asked the girl.

"My friends and I were at the mall one day, and this woman came up to me and asked if I'd ever considered modeling," the girl said.

"And what made you think she was a legitimate modeling agent?" asked the anchorwoman.

"She didn't ask all of us. Just me. She said I had the right look, and she gave me her business card. It all seemed very professional."

"What happened next?"

"She said that she was part of a team from New York that was in town for the weekend scouting for talent, and that if I was interested, I should talk to my parents and then come to this hotel for head shots and to sign with the agency."

"Which you did?"

The girl nodded. "I got my mom to take me later that afternoon. They had a whole suite, and there was all this photography equipment and a stylist and a photographer's assistant. They had me dress up in different outfits and they took my picture. And then the agent gave me a contract, and my mom read it. She said it sounded okay and I could sign it."

"What did the contract say?"

"My mom read it, so I don't really know. All she told me was that if the modeling agency got me any jobs, they would get a percentage of what I earned. Which sounded fair."

"Only they never got you any jobs?" the anchorwoman said.

The girl shook her head. "None. We waited for a while, and then called the agency a couple of times, and they said that business was slow and they would be in touch as soon as anything came up that they thought I was right for."

"Did they ever call?"

"No."

"Okay," said the anchorwoman. "Let's go back to the day you were discovered, so to speak. How much did you have to pay for those head shots?"

"About seven hundred dollars."

"Were there any other fees?"

"Yes. Three hundred and fifty for the stylist to do my hair and makeup. And two hundred dollars for the contract processing fee and my credentials."

"What did they mean by credentials?"

"Like all the information about me that went on the back of

the head shots, and a business card with my photo and contact information and the agency name on it."

"A business card that it turns out you could have ordered yourself for under twenty-five dollars?" the anchorwoman said.

The girl nodded.

"In fact, you and your mom did some research to figure out what all this would have cost had you done it on your own?"

"Yes," the girl said. "We figured out that we could have done it all for about four hundred dollars."

"And yet, you were charged well over a thousand?"

"Uh-huh," said the girl.

The image on my computer screen swiveled around as Roman aimed her webcam back at herself. "Seen enough?"

I was stunned. A scam? A modeling agent stopping girls in malls? A photographer and his crew from New York taking over a hotel suite?

"It has to be a mistake. It doesn't sound like Dad. He doesn't go around renting hotel suites. He's got his own studio here in town."

"Didn't you once tell me he goes away a lot on the weekends?"

"But that's to shoot weddings and parties."

"You're sure?"

Was I sure? The question hovered invisibly between us.

No, I wasn't.

Not anymore.

chapter 12

I TOLD ROMAN I'd talk to her later. For a second I wanted to run downstairs and ask Dad about the story, but my brain was still fuzzy from lack of sleep, and I decided to shower and dress first. Before I went downstairs, I peeked out at the street. The crowd of media people was back. There may even have been a few more reporters than the day before. And a police car had showed up to keep the street clear.

When I entered the kitchen, Mom was standing at the counter with a mug of coffee, gazing out the window at the backyard. The leaves had started to turn, and a few yellow ones were already lying on the grass. The kitchen TV was off. I poured myself some coffee.

"There was something on TV this—"

"I know," she said tersely.

The kitchen grew quiet. Mom stared out, unmoving. I'd seen her get like this before when she was really upset. Like everything had shut down except the gears churning in her brain.

"Where's Dad?" I finally asked.

"He left early."

I had to assume he'd done that to avoid the media circus outside.

"Is it true?" I asked. "I mean, about finding girls in malls and charging all that money and promising them modeling work?"

Mom turned to me. I guess I shouldn't have been surprised to see that her eyes were red, but I was.

"I think you'll have to ask him that yourself."

I took out my BlackBerry and called, but I got Dad's voice mail. The sense of discomfort I was feeling deepened. He always answered when I called. Always. I turned to Mom. Even though it was obvious she wasn't in the mood to talk, I had to ask: "You still believe he had nothing to do with the missing girls?"

She gazed at me with numb, empty eyes—the expression of someone who'd been disappointed and hurt too many times.

"I'm sorry, Mom. You don't have to answer that."

She nodded and gazed out the back window again. I couldn't help imagining those naïve, starstruck wannabes handing over the money they'd hoarded from years of babysitting, in the hope that Dad could turn them into supermodels. The dream of being on the cover of *Vogue* and flying around the world in private jets.

The thought made me wince. If the story the girl told on TV was true, it made Dad worse than a scam artist. It made him a con man and a deceiver of innocent young girls. And Janet and Gabriel had to be in on it, too, didn't they? I felt my jaw tense and a headache begin to blossom. *Please don't be true*, I prayed.

Dad couldn't have done that, could he? And not just to those girls, but to Mom and me?

My BlackBerry vibrated. I picked it up, desperately hoping it was a message from Dad.

But it wasn't.

It was vengeance13773288@gmail.com: **Enjoying the news? Hows it feel 2 have a father like that?**

chapter 13

A WAVE OF wretchedness crashed through me, filling my eyes with tears as I realized what the e-mail meant. Not just a cruel, hateful taunt to me, it was a reflection of how most of Soundview was feeling that morning. Even if they hadn't seen the interview, they would soon hear about it from friends and neighbors. By lunchtime, everyone would believe Dad was the worst kind of scoundrel.

Mom put her hand on my arm. "What is it?"

"My anonymous e-mailer again." I handed her the Black-Berry and rubbed the tears away.

The lines in Mom's forehead deepened as she studied the message from vengeance13773288@gmail.com. "How many does this make?"

"Three."

The doorbell rang. Mom's eyes met mine, and I knew we were both assuming the same thing: the media was back, no doubt eager to see how we were reacting to this morning's news.

Mom started toward the hall, saying, "I'll tell them to go away."

I sat alone in the kitchen, fearful of what the day would be like now that the whole world believed my father was not only a suspect in the disappearance of three girls but a con man as well. It might not have been so hard to cope with if I'd believed that he'd been falsely accused of the modeling scam, but something about it—some small part of it—felt ominously true. I truly, *truly* believed that he'd never hurt anyone and couldn't possibly have had anything to do with those missing girls. But I couldn't say the same about the scam.

My stomach twisted and churned. How could I reconcile the loving, protective father with the loathsome criminal everyone now thought him to be?

The kitchen door opened, and I expected to see Mom return. But Roman came in.

"What are you doing here?" I asked, surprised.

She looked somber. "Wasn't sure you'd want to go to school today, but I figured if you did, you'd want some company."

My eyes instantly filled with tears of gratitude, and I hugged her. "You are the best."

Roman had walked over, so we got into my car. With the windows raised and the doors locked, I drove down the driveway toward the waiting crowd. The media collected in the street when we got close, but the police officer got out of his car and made them clear a path so that we could pass. Some of the photographers took shots of us through the windows.

"Oh, I almost forgot," Roman said. "It's not all bad news." She propped her iPad in her lap and turned it on.

I glanced over and saw that she'd loaded a page from the *Soundview Snoop*. "Read it to me?"

"The headline is 'Rush to Judgment?' and it's by Whitman Sturges," Roman said, then read: "With the recent revelation that three missing young women from the Northeast were all clients of a local photography and modeling agency here, many in Soundview have been quick to accuse the agency's owner, Kirby Sloan, of being involved in the case. But where is the evidence to support that assumption? As Mr. Sloan's daughter, Shelby, pointed out in an exclusive interview, 'My father's entire reputation . . . my family's whole life . . . is on the line. And except for some head shots, there hasn't been a shred of evidence linking my dad to the disappearance of those girls.' Soundview's chief of police, Samuel Jenkins, has confirmed this, saying that while there has been a great deal of media attention on the case, his department has found no reason to believe that Mr. Kirby is involved. 'There are ongoing investigations in Hartford, Trenton, and Scranton regarding the missing girls,' he said. 'We've been in touch with those police departments. But so far there's been nothing that indicates that Kirby Sloan had anything to do with this.' When asked if his department had any plans to investigate Mr. Sloan's connection to the missing girls, Chief Jenkins said, 'We're letting those other departments take the lead. If they come to us with information we feel we need to act on, we will. But until then, it's important to remember that people are presumed innocent until proven guilty. Our detectives have spoken to Mr. Kirby, and, as of now, we have no reason to go any further.'"

I was shrouded by that awful guilt that comes when you've been mean to someone who was only trying to do something nice for you. Not only had I been too hard on Whit the night before, but I'd also completely misread his intentions. But then, I didn't know at that time that he was going to write an article like this.

"Uh, Shelby?" Roman said. "There's a stop sign."

I jammed on the brakes, and the tires screeched as we lurched to a stop.

"Sorry," I said.

"You didn't tell me you gave this guy an exclusive interview," Roman said.

"I didn't know I had." I explained how Whit had caught me by surprise the night before. And how I'd gotten angry and blown him off once I realized what he was up to.

"Think you owe him an apology?" she asked as I started to drive again.

"No and yes. I mean, I'd like to thank him for what he wrote, but all I knew last night was that he was looking for information for an article. Maybe if he'd told me what he was planning, I would have been a little more understanding."

"Are journalists supposed to tell you ahead of time what they're planning to write?" Roman switched off the iPad.

It was a rhetorical question, and neither of us spoke as I drove the rest of the way to school. I wondered if Roman was thinking what I was thinking: Whit had obviously written his article before the story about "the alleged" modeling scam appeared on TV. Given this morning's revelations, would he still have defended my father? And would Chief Jenkins still have said all that politically correct stuff about being innocent until proven guilty?

But wasn't I doing exactly what I was so angry at everyone else for doing? Judging Dad based on no real evidence? Just because some girl on TV said he was running a modeling scam, did that mean it was true?

No, not necessarily.

Innocent until proven guilty.

Right?

Usually.

But as soon I stepped through the front doors, it was obvious that at school the verdict was already in.

THE STARES AND whispers were everywhere. As Roman and I walked past the main office, even the secretaries paused in what they were doing. I felt Roman nudge me. Chris Clarke was coming down the hall. I steeled my nerves and decided to do what Roman suggested and say something.

"You go, girl," she whispered as I headed toward him.

But I didn't make it. Halfway there, my eyes met his, and he instantly looked away. No smile. No nod.

I felt a chill and rejoined Roman.

"What happened?" she asked in a low voice.

"He's not interested anymore," I said, feeling like I wanted to cry.

"What are you talking about? He—"

"Stop." I cut her short, not wanting to discuss it. "You didn't see what I saw. He's not interested, period. End of discussion."

Roman slid her arm through mine. "I'm sorry, Shels; that really sucks."

I fought back tears. *Yes,* I thought. *It really does.*

By lunchtime I'd called Dad three times, but he hadn't answered. It was so unlike him that I even tried the studio number, hoping Janet or Mercedes would get him for me. But all I got was voice mail.

"No appetite?" Roman asked in the cafeteria at lunch.

I shook my head. The thought of eating made me ill.

"Talk to your dad?"

I told her about the unanswered calls. "I'm worried that something bad has happened."

"Why don't you go over to the studio?"

The idea hadn't occurred to me. "You mean, right now? Just leave school?"

"I told you this morning I was kind of amazed you wanted to come here in the first place."

I thought about it and, without realizing what I was doing, let my gaze drift around the cafeteria. For what felt like the first time that day, not one person was staring in my direction. They were all eating and talking with friends. I don't know why my gaze stopped where it did, at a table filled with girls. Maybe because Ashley Walsh, an old friend of mine, was sitting there. And now I looked at the girls she was currently friendly with: Emily Bryson, Sonja Dean, and Tara Kraus, the girl who'd called Dad a creep the day before.

Just at that moment, Tara looked up. When she realized my eyes were on her, she wrinkled her nose and gave me the most hateful look imaginable. Then she said something to the other girls at the table, and they all stared at me.

I quickly looked away, but my mind was made up. Given the choice between getting hateful stares or going to the studio to see if Dad was okay, I chose the latter.

"I'm out of here." I got up.

Roman gave me a quick hug. "Let me know what you find out, okay?"

It felt strange to walk out of school in the middle of the day, almost as if I expected one of the principals to come running out to ask where I thought I was going. But no one did.

A few minutes later, as I drove down the street toward the studio, the mob of media people camped outside began to mobilize. Camera strobes flashed, and one guy with a microphone made a cranking motion as if he wanted me to lower my window. I looked for Whit in the crowd but didn't see him.

In addition to the regular collection of cars, two dark sedans were parked in the lot behind the studio. The police had returned. Maybe that explained why Dad hadn't answered my calls that morning.

I rang the back-door bell and waited a long time before Mercedes answered. She tried to smile, but you could see the stress in her eyes.

"*La policía está aquí?*" I whispered as I stepped inside.

"Yes."

"*¿Cómo estás?*" I asked.

She blinked, as if surprised that I'd be concerned about her, considering what was going on with my father, then nodded silently.

"This must be so upsetting for you."

"More for you than for me," she replied.

"I don't have a little boy to support."

Her gaze quickly dropped. The new allegations didn't affect just Mom and me. They affected everyone who worked at the studio. "I'll be okay," she said.

I wondered how true that was. Mercedes needed this job. She didn't have a husband to help raise her son and support her. Each day, a rotating cast of men with tattoos and earrings driving low-riding growly cars would drop her off at work. I had no idea whether they were brothers, cousins, or . . . boyfriends?

Janet came around the corner, looking agitated. She walked toward us with her head down, rummaging through her bag and muttering to herself until she looked up and abruptly stopped with an expression of surprise on her face. It was a strange moment, and I had the distinct feeling that she was apprehensive about what I might do or say.

"Hi," I said.

A second passed when she seemed to gather herself. "He's in the office," she said, then pulled a pack of cigarettes from her bag and went outside.

chapter 15

I WALKED DOWN the hall toward the studio office, wondering if I'd run into Gabriel next and how he'd react to seeing me. And how I'd react to seeing him after bolting out of his apartment the night before. But I got to the office, and inside, Dad was leaning against a desk with his arms crossed while two men in sports jackets sorted through files. He saw me, said something to the men, then came out.

"Sorry I couldn't answer your calls, sweetheart," he said. "These guys have been here all morning."

"What's going on?" I whispered.

Dad nodded across the hall to the photo studio, where we could speak in private. Inside, we stood in a corner beside a small sink, refrigerator, and espresso machine.

"They showed up with a warrant to go through the files again," he said while putting a pod in the espresso machine.

"But Chief Jenkins said you weren't a suspect."

"Just because they're looking at files doesn't mean I'm a suspect in a crime. At this point we don't even know if there's *been* a crime. They're probably just looking for more information about the missing girls. Want a cup?"

He carried two espressos over to a table and we sat.

"What about that girl on TV this morning?" I asked.

Dad ran his fingers through his hair. "We're always on the lookout for new talent. Everybody in this business is."

"But she said you charged much more."

"It's costly, sweetheart. The transportation . . . putting everyone up in the hotel. So we have to charge more for head shots than some local photographer with a studio in his garage. But what they didn't say on TV this morning is we give them a lot more for their money. It's not just the head shots. Any hack with a Nikon can charge rock-bottom prices for that. We're a full-service agency. We can give these girls entrée into the modeling world that no hack can match."

I understood what he was saying, but there was something else. "But the girl on TV this morning said you never got her any jobs. Have you ever taken money from a girl who you knew had no chance of becoming a model?"

The skin around Dad's eyes tightened. "Seriously, Shels? It's not my job to judge who can and can't be a model. That's for magazine editors and ad directors to decide. My job is to give girls the best shot I can. I mean, if they want to give modeling a try, who am I to stop them?"

"What about the girls Janet approached in a mall?" I asked. "What about the ones who never even *thought* about being models until she gave them her card and told them she thought they could do it?"

Dad placed a hand flat on the table and looked off. "Come on, sweetheart, doesn't *every* girl dream of being a model at some point? That's not an idea Janet put in their heads for the first time."

I sipped my espresso and stared down at the tabletop, feeling my face grow warm with frustration. Did he really expect me to accept that explanation? Did he think I was that stupid? Or naïve? The more I thought about it, the more upset I felt. I didn't want to hear his rationales and justifications, just like I didn't want him to be a man who preyed on young girls. But if that's what he was, I just wished he'd come out and admit it. The fact that he couldn't be honest with me hurt. My eyes began to well up with tears. I sniffed, wiped them away, and stared across the photo studio at the autographed photos on the wall, unable to look at him. "Dad, please just tell me the truth."

He finished his espresso, turned the little cup upside down on the saucer, and sighed. "Okay, Shels, you want the truth? Maybe we did stretch it a little with some of the girls to cover our expenses. But think about who I was doing it for—for us. For our family, our house, our cars, our vacations, clothes, you name it. . . . You have no idea how much money it takes to live the way we do."

"Couldn't you have just told us to cut back?" I asked. "Mom and I would have done it in an instant."

Dad spun the little cup around in the saucer. The rattling sound echoed through the empty studio. "You mean, admit I was a failure?"

That caught me by surprise. "No! You're not a failure. You're a success. You're amazing. You take beautiful pictures. You run a photo studio and a modeling agency. I mean—" I waved my hand toward the photos of successful models and actors whose careers he'd helped launch. "I mean, look at the people you've worked with."

Dad snorted derisively. "Past performance is no guarantee of future results."

"You should have *told* us," I said, feeling terrible. "I don't need to live in a big house with a swimming pool. I don't even need to have a car."

"And college?" Dad asked.

"I'll go to the state university."

Dad hung his head. "Maybe you're right. Maybe I should have told you. I just . . . It's not like we set out to con anyone. It just . . . happened . . . gradually. First it was one girl. Then two. Then a few each weekend. The money was coming in, and after a while we just stopped thinking about it."

"What about Janet and Gabriel?" I asked. "They had to be in on it, too, right?"

Dad shrugged. "Janet probably noticed that I wasn't turning anyone away, so she got less discriminating about who she picked. She knew that before I could pay her, I had to cover the travel and hotel expenses, and that the more girls she chose, the more chance there was that she'd make money. I mean, we were working weekends, Shels. People expect to make some money."

He gave me a quizzical glance, as if my reaction was important. Then he added. "I made a mistake. I'm sorry, sweetheart. I truly am."

73

It may have been strange to feel relief at a moment like that, but I did. I put my hand on his and squeezed it. "Dad, everyone makes mistakes. I can forgive you for that. I'm just glad you told me the truth."

His eyes got glittery. "Thank you, sweetheart. You're the best. I love you."

"I love you, too, Dad."

WAS I DISAPPOINTED? Yes. Did I feel Dad had let me down? Yes. There was no way around the fact that he'd been dishonest. But misleading those girls—even making promises he couldn't keep—was a far cry from physically harming anyone. Now that I had the answer I'd needed, it would be best not to get marked absent from my afternoon classes. I'd just let myself out the back studio door when Gabriel drove into the parking lot. I braced myself. He'd gone on those weekend "fishing" trips with Dad and had seen the girls who'd come to the hotel for head shots. So he, too, had been in on the scam.

He stopped his car and lowered the window. "Hey."

"Hi," I said, deliberately monotone.

He tilted his head at the green sedans. "The cops again?"

I nodded. Gabriel gave me a long searching look, which made me feel uncomfortable.

"I have to get back to school," I said.

"Wait. I *really* have to talk to you." He got out and shoved his hands into his pockets. The breeze played with his hair. "Look, I just want to say I'm sorry."

"For . . . ?" As much as I didn't want it to, a little part of me inside started to melt.

"What we did." He tilted his head at the studio. "And for coming on a little too strong last night. For everything. . . . It's just that I've kind of . . . liked you for a really long time, but because I work for your dad . . . and because of what was going on here with the head shots . . . I didn't feel like I could do anything about it." He gave me another searching look. "You understand, don't you?"

I nodded. It was what I'd always suspected. He'd been wary about getting involved with the boss's daughter. Plus, he hadn't wanted to be in the position of dating someone from whom he would have to keep the secret of Dad's scam.

He put his hand on my arm. "So maybe . . . now that you know . . . if you still felt like it, we could see each other one of these days?"

I felt myself stiffen. Even as attracted to him as I felt, I'd have to think hard about that. He'd been part of the scam. Part of something that was unseemly and unethical, if not outright illegal. It was one thing to forgive Dad, whom I loved. But it was something else entirely to get emotionally involved with a guy who was capable of doing what he'd done. "I . . . I need to think about it," I said honestly. "But I really appreciate everything you just said. Really. We'll talk later, okay?"

Most people react to good news in the same way. But you can learn a lot about someone by how they react to bad news. Gabriel didn't appear annoyed or resentful. Instead, he accepted what I

said and even seemed a little regretful. "Yeah, I guess I understand." He pursed his lips and gazed away.

He looked sad, and suddenly, I felt the urge to kiss him. Not
on the lips, but just a peck on the cheek, which I did. "Hey, I
didn't say no. I just said I needed to think."

The peck and the words clearly caught him by surprise. He
looked up and gave me a sheepish grin. "All right . . . Thanks."

Back at school I didn't see Roman until study hall in the library
last period.

"What happened?" she asked.

Even though she was my best friend, I didn't feel comfortable
telling her everything I'd learned. It was too personal. So I gave
her an edited version—about how Dad had to charge more for his
head shots because of the travel expenses involved, but how his
agency offered the girls much more in terms of helping them get
into the modeling business, and how it wasn't his job to decide
who could be a model or not.

"Hmmm." It was a relief to hear her hum and know that she
had something else on her mind. "I've been reading about serial
killers."

I rolled my eyes. "Those girls are probably still alive somewhere. And they live hundreds of miles away from each other."

"Exactly," Roman said, as if that was an argument for and not
against her idea. "That's the way serial killers work. In a broad
geographical area so that the police in all those different towns
won't connect the dots."

"You are whacked."

"I am *serious*."

Sometimes she could really be exasperating. "Seriously, Romy? My guess is that if you study *every* serial killer who's ever lived, you're bound to find one who operated in whatever way fits your latest theory. I mean, there's probably a serial killer who wore a chicken suit. And one who only killed on Thursdays. And what about the famous vegan killer who only killed people who ate meat?"

Roman harrumphed. "Forget it, Shelby. Just remember, when it turns out that I'm right, I'll be glad to accept your apology."

I couldn't deal with this right now. Not after the day I'd had. "Can we please talk about something else?"

She doodled on the cover of one of her notebooks. "You know, there's a party at Courtney Rajwar's on Saturday."

"Not interested."

"What are you going to do all weekend?"

"How about hide?"

Roman rolled her eyes disapprovingly. The bell rang. School was over, and she started to pack up her books. When I stayed seated, she said. "You're not going home?"

"Not yet."

"What are you waiting for?"

"Everyone else to leave. Just wait ten minutes?"

"Oh, I can't," she said. "When you left school before? I didn't know if you were coming back, so I asked David Curlin for a ride."

She left, and I read *InStyle* until I thought most of the kids had gone. Then I went out to the parking lot. There were still plenty of cars around, mostly belonging to kids on the various sports teams. Because I'd left school at lunch and then returned, I'd had to park my car in a far corner of the lot, in a spot where some low-hanging pine trees cast deep shadows. It was a place that was hard to see from the school building and, as a result, flattened cigarette butts were scattered around the asphalt.

I was lost in thought about Dad and how, even though he'd admitted that those "fishing trips" were at least partly a scam, it was important to remember that for many of the girls who had gotten their head shots from him, it was completely legitimate.

There had to be some girls who'd gotten modeling jobs, right?

I wished I'd asked Dad about that.

That's what I was thinking when I got to my car . . . and felt a presence behind me.

chapter 17

I SPUN AROUND.

It was Whit. He stopped when he saw me jump.

"Sorry," he apologized. "Didn't mean to scare you."

My heart fluttered, but unlike the fluttering it did for Gabriel, this was caused by fright. I hadn't realized how jumpy I was.

"What are you doing here?" I asked. Nonstudents weren't allowed on school property.

"Trying not to partake in pack journalism." He saw the scowl on my face and explained: "It's when they all bunch up and go after a story together. Like those crowds that hang out in front of your house and your father's studio every day."

That reminded me of something. "Thanks for writing that article about not rushing to judgment about my dad. As far as I know, you're the only one who's said anything in defense of him."

"You're welcome."

"And . . . I'm sorry I threatened to call the police."

He grinned. "I probably would have done the same thing."

"Only now that you know what was on the news this morning, I bet you regret what you wrote."

"No way," he said. "I wrote about the rush to blame him for the missing girls. I still stand by that."

There was something honest and disarming about him that made me want to talk. "Can we go off the record?"

Whit's lips parted into a wry smile. "All right. What's up?"

"What do you know about serial killers?"

A few lines between his eyebrows bunched. "Not much."

"You know why I'm asking, right?"

"Sure. And if it turns out that one's involved in this case? I won't be totally surprised."

"You won't?" I replied, caught off guard by his answer. "But no one knows what's up with those girls. They could still be alive."

Whit studied me. "You really believe that?"

He was right. "It's seriously wishful thinking, isn't it?" I admitted.

Whit nodded. "Off the record. I'll tell you something . . . if you swear not to share it with anyone."

"Okay."

"I've spoken to either the family or friends of all three girls. Everyone's willing to talk because they hope that the more news there is and the more times those girls' photos are shown, the more likely it is that someone will recognize one of them or know something helpful. The common thread that comes out is that none of them was having problems at home or was in any kind of situation that would make you think they'd want to run away.

I mean, not that life was perfect or anything, but two of them have serious boyfriends who they never said a word to about going anywhere. And the other one was totally focused on taking her GED test. She'd dropped out of high school the year before, and everyone I spoke to agreed that all she wanted in life was to get that high school diploma."

Whit paused as if he knew I needed a moment to digest what he'd said. Then he added, "That's going to be my next story."

"But won't that imply that my dad's somehow involved?" I asked.

His eyebrows dipped as if he didn't see the connection. "I don't even plan to mention him in the article. All I'm going to say is that, based on the interviews I've done, it appears unlikely that the girls ran away."

I felt myself getting upset. "Everyone already thinks my father's the number one suspect, and now you're going to write a story that says they weren't the kind of girls who'd run away. So that implies that something bad must have happened to them. It's just going to make it worse for my dad." I almost added, *Especially after this morning's news from that girl claiming Dad was running a scam*, but I decided against it.

"I honestly don't think people will see it that way," Whit said.

"Oh, come off it," I snapped angrily. "You and I both know that's *exactly* the way they'll see it!"

Whit didn't reply. He just stood there like a big dumb galoot. I got into my car, slammed the door, and peeled out of the parking lot.

* * *

Mom wasn't home when I got there, so I went online to check the latest developments. There was nothing new in the local news, and I was secretly glad to see that the papers in Scranton and Trenton had beaten Whit to the story about the girls not being the type to want to run away. Good, maybe he'd give up on becoming a journalist and go away.

When I heard the back door open downstairs, I went down to the kitchen. Mom was sitting at the table, reading the *Soundview Gazette*. I glanced at the oven and realized there was a frozen pizza inside. It was hard to remember the last time she hadn't prepared dinner herself.

"Hey, what's up?" I asked.

"How was your day?" she asked back.

"Difficult." I told her how I'd gone to the studio at lunch and had seen the detectives going through Dad's files. And how Dad had admitted that Janet looked for modeling prospects at the malls and sometimes picked girls who didn't really have a chance at a career. "Dad said he did it for us."

"What?" Mom's voice shook with consternation.

"He was trying to make enough money so that we could live the way we do," I said. "That's true, isn't it? I mean, about his not being able to make enough money from the work he gets in the studio? Two days ago, he was doing a Chinese food menu."

Mom made an odd motion with her head. "I suppose."

"I just wish he'd said something to us. I don't have to have my own car. I could have done with less. I guess men are funny that way. If he couldn't make enough to support us, it was like admitting he was a failure."

Mom sighed mysteriously. I wished she'd tell me what she was thinking. It wasn't like she was protecting me from some terrible truth by not sharing her feelings.

The kitchen phone rang. Mom studied the readout, then picked up the receiver. "Yes? Uh-huh. Okay." She hung up and turned to gaze out the kitchen window. By now it was dark, and all I imagined she could see were the streetlights.

"Mom? What was it?" I asked.

Without turning she said, "Your father. They're taking him to the police station . . . for questioning."

chapter 18

THE NEWS WAS jolting. "Questioning? But yesterday, Chief Jenkins said he wasn't a suspect. He said they had no evidence. . . ."

Mom didn't answer. It was understandable, since she probably knew no more than I did. But I had to believe that something about the investigation had changed. With all those police departments and media people involved, new information must have been turning up all the time. Just because Dad hadn't been a suspect yesterday was no reason to think he couldn't be one today. Once again, I felt my eyes grow watery.

"I don't understand," I said anxiously. "I mean, Dad might have done some things wrong, but he can't actually be a suspect in the disappearance of these girls, can he? I mean . . . seriously, Mom, can't you tell me what you really think?"

The timer in the oven binged and seemed to snap her out of a trance. She pulled on some oven mitts. "Sorry, what did you say?"

I repeated what I'd said, while she sliced the pizza and took a bowl of salad out of the refrigerator. "No," she said, bringing the salad to the table. "I don't think he could really be a suspect."

She started to eat a slice of pizza while I pushed my salad around with a fork. Once again it came to me that just because we didn't think Dad could be a suspect meant nothing as far as the rest of the world was concerned.

My BlackBerry buzzed. I quickly looked, then felt a sickening sensation when I saw that it was from vengence13773288@gmail.com: **Hope ur enjoying the news. xoxo!**

Of course, I thought miserably, it was the dinner hour—the start of the nightly news cycle. Placing the BlackBerry on the table where Mom could read it, I reached for the remote and turned on the TV. But whatever the anonymous e-mailer had been writing about wasn't on the local news, and I had to surf until I found it on a network channel, where a reporter was speaking to a young blonde woman named Destiny Charles.

Destiny was cuter than the girl who'd been on TV that morning. At first her story sounded the same as the one we'd heard before: she'd been approached in a mall by a woman claiming to be a modeling agent. Later that day, she'd gone to the hotel with her mother and paid a lot for the styling, head shots, and credentials.

"I guess now that one channel's found a girl who fell for the scam, every channel has to have one," I said bitterly.

But I was wrong. There was more.

"So what happened after that?" the interviewer asked.

"About a week later, Mr. Sloan called and said he thought he had a modeling job for me, but he wanted to meet and talk about it first," Destiny said.

"And what did you say?"

"I asked if my mom could come."

"And what did Mr. Sloan say?"

"He said it would be better if we met alone."

I felt myself start to tighten up. *Oh no. Oh God, please, no!*

"Did you ask why?"

Destiny nodded. "He said that he wanted to see how I acted on my own, without my mom there, because they were looking for a girl who projected maturity and independence, and that sometimes when girls were with their moms, they acted more like daughters."

"So did you meet him alone?" the interviewer asked.

Destiny shook her head. "I was scared. It didn't sound right. I mean, if he wanted to see how I acted alone, why couldn't my mom bring me and then wait outside or something?"

"Did you suggest that?"

"No. I didn't think of that until later. I was too nervous on the phone."

"So something about the idea felt wrong to you?"

"I wasn't sure. I mean, it could have been true that I didn't act as mature when my mom was around. I just didn't know."

"But something about it felt wrong?" the interviewer repeated.

Suddenly realizing that I'd been holding my breath, I let it out. "She's putting words in her mouth. She's trying to get her to say it felt wrong."

Mom watched silently.

"I didn't know," Destiny said again. "I guess I just didn't want to take a chance."

The interviewer thanked her and the camera shifted to an anchor behind a desk.

"So I guess we'll never really know why the photographer Kirby Sloan wanted to meet Destiny Charles alone," the anchor said.

"I spoke to several photographers at well-established studios, and none of them thought it sounded right," the interviewer replied. "Most of them couldn't think of a reason why the girl couldn't have been asked to project maturity while her mother was there."

The anchor nodded but didn't comment. Thus, the last idea left in everyone's mind was what the interviewer had implied—that other photographers thought Dad's reason for wanting to see Destiny alone sounded dubious.

The show went to a commercial, and I muted the TV.

"That doesn't prove anything," I said. "All that girl said was that Dad wanted to meet her alone. We don't even know if she's telling the truth. Maybe she made the whole thing up just to get on TV. People do that all the time. Or maybe she didn't understand what Dad meant."

I waited for Mom to say something, but once again she seemed to be gone. As if her mind was a million miles away. "Mom?"

She turned to me and blinked. "You're right, dear, it doesn't prove anything."

I studied her tired face. "You're not just saying that, right? I mean, to protect me?"

"From what?"

"From the truth," I said, puzzled that she didn't seem to understand.

"The truth," she repeated woodenly.

Suddenly, I felt a new concern. Was this all too much for her? For years she'd been pretending that everything in our family was perfect and that we were just like every other family. Was she coming apart, just as our world was?

chapter 19

"MOM, ARE YOU okay?" I asked.

Her expression changed, as if she realized I was studying her. She reached for the salad tongs and placed some greens on her plate. "Of course I am, darling. It's just . . . this is . . . you know . . . a difficult time." She picked up a slice of pizza and offered it to me. "But don't worry, we'll get through it. Another slice?"

I accepted the slice even though I knew I didn't have the appetite to take more than a few bites.

"I was thinking that maybe we'd have a dinner party the weekend before Thanksgiving," Mom said. "Invite the neighbors, you know?"

It felt like time for a major reality check. Dad was being questioned by the police, and Mom was talking about a party? Did she really think the neighbors would want to come, given the awful news surrounding our family? Only if by then this whole mystery about the girls was cleared up and Dad's innocence was proven.

Mom was counting on that.

So was I.

We talked about whom we could invite. Because my parents hardly went out, they didn't have a lot of friends in Soundview. There were some neighbors like the Sisks, and some women Mom met for book club every Thursday. For the most part, Dad's friends were the same ones he'd had back when he worked in the city.

After dinner I put the unfinished salad and pizza in the refrigerator, in case Dad was hungry when he got home. Back upstairs it was hard not to go online, but I really didn't want to communicate with anyone. As I did my homework, I kept expecting a text from Roman, and I was surprised when none arrived. Had she not heard the news? Had she heard it and was trying to be sensitive? Or had she gone out? After all, it was Friday.

Later I heard the back door open downstairs and knew Dad was home. I found him in the kitchen pouring tequila into a shot glass.

"Hey, sweetheart." He looked and sounded worn out.

"Hi, Dad." I knew I sounded glum.

He took a sip. "Guess I don't have to ask what's wrong."

"What did the police want to know?"

"What you'd expect," he said. "Did I have anything to do with the missing girls? Did I know anything about why they were missing? Did I have any idea where they were? That kind of stuff. Don't worry, I passed. Questions, lie-detector test, whole nine yards."

"Lie detector?" I repeated, surprised.

He took a long sip and, despite his obvious fatigue, winked

mischievously. He'd passed! He was innocent! For a split second I felt an urge to throw my arms around his neck, but the memory of what I'd seen earlier on TV stopped me. "Dad, while you were down at the police station? There was something on TV. A girl who you signed up for modeling. She said you wanted to meet her alone."

Dad's eyebrows rose curiously. "No kidding? Did they say why?"

"No, but it was kind of implied."

He scowled for an instant as if he didn't understand, then smirked as if he did. "Ah, the old casting-couch routine. And where was this alleged assignation supposed to take place?"

"She didn't say," I said.

Dad nodded as if he wasn't surprised, then took another sip. "So she said I wanted to meet her alone, but the meeting never took place." He shook his head. "Talk about kicking a guy when he's down."

I almost said, "So it's not true?" But it was obvious from the way Dad was acting that it wasn't.

He gazed up at the ceiling with a reflective expression. "Know what? I can't say I blame them."

I stared at him in shock. "*What?* Why?"

"Because it's business, sweetheart. TV stations make money by selling ads. And to sell ads, they need viewers; and to get viewers, they have to have a good story. And even when you've got a good story, you better have some new twist on it every evening at six, or the viewers are going to switch channels until they find a station that does."

He was right, of course. That's exactly what I'd done at dinner—switched channels until I found the one with the story about this girl who claimed Dad wanted to meet her alone.

"It's sick," I said.

"Yeah, well, it's also life," he said in a resigned tone. "Better get used to it."

It was getting late, and I was exhausted from the accumulated stresses of the past days, so I kissed Dad on the cheek and went upstairs. Basically, the news was good. Dad was innocent as far as those missing girls were concerned. Feeling better about his situation, I decided to go online. It turned out that Roman had just gotten on, and I told her how Dad had passed the lie-detector test.

"But you know they're not reliable," she said. "You see them on TV and in the movies because it's dramatic, but you can't convict someone just because they failed a lie-detector test."

"But Dad didn't fail, he passed."

"Same difference. Just because you pass doesn't mean you're innocent. They probably gave it to him to see how he'd react. Like maybe he'd get scared and confess on the spot. That's happened, you know. And I mean, you can go online and learn about ways to beat a lie detector."

"I'm sure Dad didn't do that," I said. "He didn't even know they were going to give him the test until he got to the police station."

"Hmmm." Roman made that sound, and I knew she was going to change the subject. "So . . . I . . . saw that girl Destiny on TV before. I mean, I understand totally if you don't want to talk about it."

I felt my face grow warm. "She admitted that nothing happened. You don't even know if she's telling the truth."

"You think she'd just make it up?" Roman asked.

It was strange how, when Dad had scoffed at the idea, I'd been so eager to believe that Destiny was just looking for publicity. But now that Roman asked the question, the publicity angle felt less likely.

"I don't know," I admitted.

"Maybe you're right," Roman said. "If nothing happened, maybe it doesn't matter."

But I felt my spirits go into a free fall. "It's still bad news heaped on bad news."

On the screen, Roman sighed sympathetically. "I think we should go out and have fun tomorrow."

"I don't know if I can, Romy."

"Right, Shels. Which is exactly why you *should*. You can't spend the whole weekend hiding in your house."

"So what would you suggest?"

Roman held up a credit card and gave me a big smile. "Go shopping, what else?"

"Not at the Soundview Mall. I don't want to spend the whole time worrying about running into people I don't want to see."

"Let's go up to Stamford," Roman suggested. "It's just as nice as Soundview, and hardly anyone from around here goes there."

She was right. The worst thing I could do was hang around the house waiting and worrying about whatever was going to happen next.

chapter 20

"YOU *HAVE TO* buy that top," Roman said at Vintage Vogue the next morning.

It was the cutest ruffled chiffon tank, and I was completely in want with it, but then I checked the price tag and shook my head.

"But it loves you, and you'll look great in it," Roman insisted.

I put it back on the rack. "Don't want to spend the money."

"Since when?"

I cocked my head and gave her a look as if to say, "Think about it."

"Oh." Roman pressed her fingers to her lips. "You mean because of what's happening?"

"It's not like Dad's doing any business," I said as we left the store. Then, even though there was no one around, I lowered my voice. "He only did what he did to make the money we needed to live the way we do. So now I feel like it's partly my fault."

"Why didn't he just tell you not to spend as much?"

"Apparently, that's not how the male ego works. The great hunter is supposed to kill enough game to feed his family."

Roman stopped. "Does the great hunter ever say what he thinks happened to those missing girls?"

"He has no idea."

"What do *you* think?" she asked.

"I think if something bad happened to them, it almost has to have something to do with Dad's business. It can't be just a coincidence. So if Dad doesn't know anything about them, then someone who works with him must. And that's a seriously scary and upsetting idea."

"That would be Gabriel, Janet, and I forget the other one's name?"

"Mercedes. Only I can't imagine what she could have to do with it. All she cares about is her little boy."

"So that leaves Gabriel or Janet."

"Exactly."

Roman gave me a sideways look as we started to walk. "What are you thinking?"

"Maybe I can get Gabriel to tell me a few things."

Roman frowned, then her eyebrows shot skyward as she realized what I was implying. "Don't tell me. Look out, Nancy Drew, here comes Shelby Sloan, girl detective?"

"I'm serious," I said.

"Seriously whacked." Her voice reeked of disapproval. "And just suppose that Gabriel really is behind those girls' disappearing. Then what?"

"I tell the police."

"Oh, sure." She chuckled caustically. "He's just going to stand by and let you do that."

"I'm not going to be obvious about it."

"I would so love to be a fly on the wall for *that* conversation," Roman said. "Only seriously, sista? If he's involved with those missing girls, you could find yourself in some very deep doo-doo."

I was about to reply that I planned to be extra careful, when I noticed a pack of girls gathered around a perfume kiosk. They were all juniors from Soundview High, and it looked as if a moment ago they'd been trying the fragrances. But now they all stared at Roman and me. Well, at me mostly. And given the recent news, it wasn't hard to figure out why.

Roman tugged at my sleeve and we turned away. "So much for going someplace where no one would know you," she muttered.

"I can't get used to people looking at me that way," I said, feeling ire rise above the other emotions churning inside me. "I mean, not only is it incredibly rude, but it feels like they're blaming *me*. Like it's *my* fault."

"It's just the way people are," Roman said. "If I were you, I'd give it right back to them."

I stopped, surprised. "Why?"

"Because every time you slink away, it looks like you're admitting guilt."

She was right. I glanced in the direction of the perfume kiosk. "Should I go back?"

"No. The moment's passed. But now that this has happened, you might as well go to the party tonight."

I stared at her. "Now, *that's* a logical segue. . . . Not."

"All I'm saying is, now that you've dealt with this, nothing worse is going to happen."

I couldn't help but smile. Sometimes Roman could be so crazy. "That has to be the most illogical thing you've ever said."

"Maybe, but that doesn't mean it isn't also true."

"You just don't want to go alone," I said.

Roman linked arms with me. "Actually, I will go alone. Because you'll go with Gabriel."

chapter 21

I ASKED ROMAN how—in less than two minutes—she'd gone from not wanting me to have anything to do with Gabriel to suggesting I invite him to the party that night.

"When I said I didn't think you should go anywhere near him, did you listen?" she asked.

I admitted I hadn't.

"Exactly," she said. "So invite him to the party. At least there'll be lots of people around, so you'll be safe, and besides, now I'm curious. I mean, how many times in life do you get to meet someone who could really be a bad guy?"

"So now I'm an excuse for your vicarious thrills?" I groaned, only half seriously.

Roman laughed. "Come on, Shels. What else are you good for?"

Later, when I called Gabriel and invited him to Courtney's party, he first sounded surprised, then mumbled something about having things to do but that he might be able to find time to drop by.

* * *

Despite Roman's weird logic, I still wasn't thrilled about going to the party, especially when the first person I saw was my old friend Ashley, who was part of Tara Kraus's posse. Ashley was a tall, pretty girl, with a red streak in her dark brown hair. She was shy and quiet until she got to know you. We'd been best friends in middle school, but then her dad lost his job and they'd had to sell their house and move into a small apartment in town. After that, she and I had drifted apart. These days, Ashley left school early to work at a nearby amusement park called Playland. Knowing she was at the party wasn't really a problem for me. The problem was that if Ashley was there, it was reasonable to expect that Tara would show up, too.

Since Tara wasn't there yet and Ashley and I were both alone, I thought it might be nice to go over and say hello. I'd just started through the crowd toward her when Gabriel strolled out of the kitchen with a beer.

"Hey, there you are." He grinned. "How come you look so surprised?"

"I . . . I just didn't think you'd get here before me."

"I got everything done faster than I thought I would," he said. He was wearing a black blazer, with a black shirt and jeans. I couldn't help noticing that, in comparison, the other guys at the party looked like schoolboys. Once again I felt people's eyes on me, but this time the girls stared with expressions of envy and curiosity.

And I wasn't the only one who was aware of the stares. So was Gabriel. He actually seemed to enjoy them. While we talked, his eyes darted about, as if keeping score of who was watching.

We'd hardly begun to speak when Roman arrived and instantly joined us.

"Looking good, Gabriel," she said, purposefully trying to sound matter-of-fact about it. "I'm Roman. We met at the Sloans' Christmas party."

"Oh, right, sure," Gabriel said, pretending he remembered her.

"So how's the modeling business?" Roman asked. "Have I seen you in anything lately?"

Gabriel recited the answer: "The Soundview Ford ad, with the young couple looking for their first minivan. The Island Savings and Loan ad for free checking. And I've done some online catalog work. JCPenney and Hanes."

"Underwear?" Roman asked eagerly while she rummaged through her bag and found her iPhone.

"Wait a minute," I said. "We're not going to search for pictures of him in his underwear, are we?"

Roman lowered the phone. "Oh, my bad, huh?"

"It's no biggie," Gabriel said. "They airbrush out all the, uh, *revealing* details."

"Is it weird?" Roman asked. "I mean, standing around in your underwear with all these people looking and taking pictures."

"You get used to it." Gabriel tilted his head back and emptied the bottle.

"You don't feel embarrassed?"

"No. As far as they're concerned, the only difference between me and a mannequin is that I have a pulse." He gestured at the empty bottle. "You girls thirsty?"

We went into the kitchen, where Gabriel took a second to check his reflection in the window, then pulled three Bud Lights out of the refrigerator and handed one each to Roman and me.

"I know it's a little flaky," he said, twisting the cap off, "but if you want to work, you have to keep the pounds off."

"You must spend a lot of time in the gym," Roman said.

"Yeah. Not my favorite place to be, but you do what you have to do."

"So what is your favorite place to be?" I asked. "I mean, other than at a poker table."

His grin turned sheepish. "Outside, in the woods. Hiking, mountain biking. That kind of thing." He paused. "Not what you expected?"

I had to admit it wasn't. Gabriel didn't seem like the outdoorsy type at all. But he kept talking about the places where he'd hiked and mountain biked, and the places he still wanted to go.

I couldn't help noticing that while Roman asked most of the questions, Gabriel directed most of his answers at me. Finally, it must have been obvious that he wanted to speak with me alone, and Roman wandered off. Gabriel and I stayed in the kitchen while others came and went, shooting glances at us while they raided the refrigerator for beers. I asked about his apartment, and he launched into a long story about playing poker online and in casinos, and how he'd learned to read his opponents' "tells." I kept waiting to see if he'd bring up the situation with Dad and the missing girls, but he seemed content to make small talk. I couldn't tell if he was purposefully avoiding the subject or simply not thinking about it. Meanwhile, he'd polished off two more beers.

Finally, after he'd pulled yet another beer from the fridge, and I saw that nobody was around, I decided to bring up the subject myself. "What do you think is going on with those missing girls?"

"The only thing I know is that it's really hurting my bank account," Gabriel said as he took a gulp.

That caught me by surprise. Of all the answers I had imagined him giving . . . how could money be the only thing he was thinking about? Didn't he care that something bad might have happened to those girls? His lack of empathy creeped me out. At that point I might not have continued talking to him were it not for my hope that if we kept speaking, he might reveal something about his part in the situation . . . *if* he'd had a part in it at all.

Unfortunately, Gabriel interpreted my continued interest as something else. To complicate things, no matter where we went in the house, other girls seemed to find an excuse for "bumping" into us so that I would feel obligated to make an introduction. I think even Gabriel grew annoyed with all the attention, because twice he suggested that we go someplace where we wouldn't be disturbed. After I brushed the suggestion aside for a second time, he started to get a little frustrated.

By then it was getting late, and when I yawned one time too many, he seemed to reach his limit and said, "Guess I'm gonna bail."

I had mixed feelings about that—part relief, part disappointment that I hadn't learned anything useful, and even a little guilty that I'd used and misled him, even if he had helped my dad mislead all those girls who'd never had a realistic chance of becoming models. Roman had already left the party, and when I looked around, I found Tara Kraus shooting a contemptuous glance at me from a couch where she was sitting with her posse.

"I think I'll go, too," I said, and then, to make sure Gabriel didn't get the wrong idea, added, "I could use a good night's sleep."

"I bet," he muttered a little sourly.

We left the party together, which probably caused more than a few tongues to wag, but I didn't care. Gabriel walked with his head bowed uncharacteristically, and I was annoyed with myself for feeling bad about him. We got to the street, and I pointed to the left. "My car's down that way."

"Mine's up there." He pointed to the right.

An awkward moment followed. I didn't want to give him the wrong impression, but I also didn't want to alienate him any more than I already had. After all, what if it turned out that he did know something useful about the missing girls? Dad and I might still need him.

I stepped close. "I'm sorry if I seemed distracted tonight. I've just got so much on my mind. I mean, about what's going on with my dad. It's hard to stop thinking about it."

Gabriel gave me an uncertain look, as if he wasn't sure whether to believe me. Feeling like I had to be more convincing, I stretched up and gave him a quick kiss on the lips. "We'll talk, okay?"

"Sure." He smiled.

A moment later I was walking down the street, trying to replay in my head everything I could remember Gabriel saying that evening, searching for any nugget of information I might have missed. But nothing came to light.

My car was parked on the dark side of the street. I was so busy thinking about Gabriel that it didn't occur to me to consider how late it was, or the darkness, or the fact that there was no one around. I was reaching for the door . . . when suddenly, I sensed someone behind me.

chapter 22

I SPUN AROUND just as a large shadowy figure came out of the dark.

I almost screamed.

Then saw that it was Whit.

"You *have* to stop sneaking up on me like this!" I gasped, pressing my hand against my heaving heart.

"Sorry," Whit said.

My fright quickly morphed into serious annoyance. "Why do you *always* do this?"

He pointed back up the street toward the house. "What was I supposed to do? Stand where you could see me and watch while you kissed that guy?"

I glanced at Courtney's brightly lit house, then back at Whit. "Is that a rhetorical question, or am I actually supposed to have an answer?"

"I don't know," he replied with a shrug. "But I admire your taste."

I wasn't only annoyed with him for scaring me. I was still angry about that article he'd wanted to write that would have implied that Dad could have been involved in the disappearances. "Thank you. And not only is he gorgeous, but he's a really sweet, nice guy, and we have a lot of fun together."

A wry smile appeared on Whit's lips. "No kidding? So I guess you don't mind that he works for your dad and probably was complicit with the whole modeling scam? Funny, but I didn't think that was the kind of guy you'd be attracted to."

I felt my face grow hot and my eyes narrow with anger, mostly because he'd so easily caught me in my lie. "You . . . ," I started to say through gritted teeth, even though I wasn't sure exactly *what* I wanted to say.

"Now, now, be nice," he cautioned with a grin. "I haven't agreed to go off the record this time."

That just made me madder. Hating how he was teasing me, I felt my hands ball into such tight fists that my nails dug into my palms. "*Why are you doing this?*"

"You know why. You told me yourself. I'm using your father's misfortunes to catapult myself into the upper echelons of journalism."

I swung my fist. Not that I actually meant to hurt him. I was really lashing out at all of it—the anger and disappointment and injustice of everything that had happened—and he just happened to be the closest target.

"Whoa!" He caught my wrist. I'd forgotten how big his hands were. My hand in his was like a doll's. I tried to yank it back, but he held it.

"Let go!" I kept struggling.

"Calm down," he said.

"Not till you let go!"

"Not till you calm down."

We'd reached a stalemate. "Then at least . . . *stop grinning!*" I shouted.

He let go. I took a step back, rubbing my wrist and breathing hard. He hung his head, the smile gone. "Sorry. I . . . I shouldn't have made light of your problems."

I nodded, even though my emotions were still on spin cycle. "I shouldn't have gotten so mad. I guess I'm sorry, too."

"Listen, you're going through a bad time. I didn't mean to be so insensitive."

Now, from out of nowhere, came the urge to cry, but I blinked hard and fought back the tears. I didn't care how empathetic and insightful he was, he was *not* going to see me cry.

"You okay?" he asked.

I nodded and felt tiny bits of tears creep out of both eyes. *Darn it!*

Whit began to pat his pockets.

"Do *not* offer me anything to wipe my eyes with!" I practically yelled. "I am *not* crying! I'm just . . . Oh, I don't know what I am." At that moment I felt so frustrated and mixed up and fragile, I just . . . wanted . . . to be held. The next thing I knew, I stepped close to him, and he put his arms around me.

And then I started to cry for real. Shoulders shaking and voice quavering, I managed to croak out, "This . . . isn't a come-on or anything. . . . I'm . . . just really upset."

"I know." He held me firmly, but gently, and reassured me that everything was going to be all right. Gradually, the wave of emotion passed, and I backed out of his arms.

I wiped my eyes while he stood and watched silently, which was exactly what I didn't want him to do. "Actually, would you do me a huge favor?" I asked. "I could really use a beer."

Whit looked back over his shoulder at Courtney's house. "Promise you'll be here when I get back?"

"I promise."

He left, and I had a chance to fix my makeup under a street-light. A few moments later he was back with two beers. We sat on the hood of a car under an almost-full moon.

"You know, it's not really about getting a job in journalism," he said. "I mean, maybe it started out that way, but now, for me, it's gone past that. It's about finding the truth. This is the first time I've ever been involved in a story that's still unfolding. Usually, you get to the event and everything's already happened, and all you're doing is reporting on what occurred. But this is so different. Nobody knows what's really going on, and in the mean-time, people's lives are at stake." He paused and took a sip, then added, "You understand that I have nothing against your dad, right? I'm just trying to find out what happened."

I nodded, thinking that wanting to know the truth was a lot better than some of those other journalists who were only look-ing for the juiciest story they could dig up, even if it might not be entirely true. "I guess we have that in common. I want the truth, too."

Another silent moment passed. The air was slightly warmer

than usual for a late October night, and a few bugs flitted around the nearest streetlight. Then I said, "Off the record?"

"Why not?" Whit replied with a chuckle.

"No, seriously, I mean it."

"Okay."

"It wasn't my father," I said. "Don't ask me for proof, because we both know I don't have it. I just know. He may have said or done inappropriate things. . . . He may have even taken money from girls who didn't have a chance of becoming models, but he wouldn't hurt a fly. There's no way he did anything bad to those girls."

Whit nodded slowly.

"You probably think I only feel that way because I'm his daughter," I continued, "but I'm also the person he's closest to in the world. And I know he couldn't have done what people think he's done."

"Okay."

"But I'd have to be stupid not to believe that all three missing girls were involved with Dad's agency and studio," I said. "And that means someone at the studio must know something."

"Including Mr. Kissy Face?"

"His name is Gabriel, and if you have to know what that was about before," I said, "it was about trying to find out what he knows."

"Like kiss and tell?" He was teasing again.

"No! Can't you be serious?"

Whit traced the rim of the beer can with his fingertip. "Okay, seriously? You really think hanging around with him is a good idea? If someone at the studio has done something to those girls, what makes you think he or she won't do anything to you? And don't assume you've narrowed it down to the people who work there."

"What do you mean?" I asked.

"It could be someone who *knows* someone who works there. You mentioned there are two women?"

"Janet and Mercedes," I said, realizing he was right. Mercedes was always riding with those men. And who knew who Janet hung out with? There could easily be more suspects. People who could have looked through the files, picked girls, and . . .

"So instead of snooping around yourself, why not let the police take care of it?" Whit asked.

"Because I think I could be in a position to find out things they can't," I said.

"Like pillow talk with Mr. Kissy Face?"

"Stop it!" I snapped, but then admitted, "Well, maybe a little, but believe me, not on any pillows."

"What if he makes it clear it's going to take more than that to get him to talk?"

"I told you, I'm not *that* kind of girl."

"Well, if you're not *that* kind of girl, then maybe you're not the kind of girl who should be involved at all," Whit said. "Maybe you should be more focused on what's happening at home."

Once again he'd caught me by surprise. I gave him an uncertain look. How would he have any idea of what was happening at home?

"Did someone say something?" I asked. "I mean, what exactly are you referring to?"

"No one said anything," Whit answered. "And you don't have to look at me like I'm clairvoyant. Now that the rumors are out about your dad hitting on young women, I have to assume that your mom is slightly less than thrilled."

That would have been true were it not for the fact that Mom had spent so many years in denial. "Listen, Whit," I said, "it's really thoughtful of you to be concerned about my family. But even off the record, that's private."

"I'm not looking for gossip," he said. "I'm just saying it would probably be safer for you, and better for all involved, if that was the direction in which you focused your attentions."

I was impressed by his intelligence, ethics, and empathy. But despite all that, I knew I had to keep trying to prove my father's innocence.

Meanwhile, Whit gazed at me with a placid, though slightly amused, expression. "You didn't listen to a thing I just said."

He was so right.

chapter 23

I WENT TO bed that night feeling better. No matter what people said about the validity of lie-detector tests, Dad had still passed. That had to count for something. And I'd learned more about Gabriel, too. He might have been beautiful to look at, but Roman was right—deep down, it appeared that he was pretty shallow. And finally, I felt better thanks to Whit, who was reassuring in his own way, reminding me that there were still people in the world who weren't just out to further their own career regardless of who they hurt.

I slept well and woke in the morning wondering if I should follow Whit's advice and spend the day trying to help my family. Maybe some good could still come out of all of this. Surely, Dad had learned a lesson. If I could get him to tell Mom that he was truly sorry for what he'd done and was ready to change his ways, perhaps I could persuade them to at least attempt to patch up their marriage.

And it was Sunday, the perfect day to do it. I stretched and reached over to my night table to check my BlackBerry.

And instantly wished I hadn't.

There was an e-mail . . . from vengance13773288@gmail
.com: **Have fun last nite? What a hunk. But w8 till U C the
news this morning. Have a gr8 day!**

Shivers burrowed through me. First: whoever was sending
me these e-mails had been at the party last night. Second: it may
have been Sunday, but there would be no rest from bad news.

Still in my pajamas, I hurried downstairs and turned on the
TV. Neither Mom nor Dad was in the kitchen. The channels
were all doing the weather or commercials, so I made coffee
and waited. Finally, one of the channels went to a reporter wearing a yellow rain slicker and standing in a wooded area blocked
by police cars and crime scene tape: "Police here in Scranton,
Pennsylvania, are reporting this morning the discovery of a badly
decomposed body in a riverbank cave just outside the bound-
aries of a state park. Scranton chief of police Edward Naughton
cautioned that it may take some time to get a positive ID, but he
did acknowledge that the body appears to fit the description of
Rebecca Parlin, an aspiring young model who disappeared from
the area about a month ago."

I slumped into a chair as the last glimmer of hope that the
missing girls were still alive dissolved into the kitchen air. Maybe
it had been a foolish hope to begin with, but until now it had felt
like a possibility, no matter how slight. And that made it feel silly
to cling to the other improbables—that maybe the other two girls
were still alive, that maybe the disappearances had nothing to do
with Dad or the people at his studio anyway.

Mom came into the kitchen in her robe, glanced at the TV as if she already knew what was on it, and poured herself a cup of coffee.

"Where's Dad?" I asked.

"He left early."

"Why?"

"Because of all those people outside."

Oh, right, of course. Now that an actual body had been found, there was probably more media than ever. Having gone straight to the kitchen, I hadn't yet looked out front that morning.

"Can't we do something?" I asked. "What if we hire a private detective to help prove Dad is innocent?"

Mom gazed at me with sad eyes. "Why do you think a private detective could find something that all these other detectives can't find?"

"Because they're all too focused on Dad," I said. "A private detective could take a different approach. Like focus on something or someone else."

"Oh, darling, I'm sure they're already doing that," Mom said, then paused and studied me as if she'd just thought of something. "It's best if we stay out of it. If your father is innocent, I'm sure they'll—"

"*If* he's innocent?" I repeated, cutting her short. "Mom, how can you say that? *Of course* he's innocent."

Mom's eyes widened as if she were as surprised by what she'd said as I was. "Oh, I'm so sorry, darling, that's not what I meant."

"You sure?" I asked.

She smiled reassuringly. "Yes."

* * *

A little later, back upstairs, I talked to Roman about the dead girl in Scranton. "This is going to turn the heat way up on my dad."

"Not necessarily," she said.

"How can you say that? He's the prime suspect. As far as I can tell, he's the *only* suspect. And like you said, lie-detector tests don't really count. The only way anyone's going to believe he's innocent is if I prove he is."

"If *you* prove it?" Roman replied, alarmed. "Wait a minute, Shels, they've found a body with her hands and feet tied up. There's a real murderer out there somewhere. This isn't Nancy Drew anymore. You *have* to stay out of this."

"But there's definitely something strange about Gabriel," I argued. "I mean, when it comes to those missing girls, he's got zero empathy. All this means to him is that he's not making any money. It's almost like he's a sociopath."

"Thanks for the diagnosis, Dr. Sloan," Roman said, making no effort to hide the sarcasm. "But if Gabriel's involved in this, I don't have to tell you why going anywhere near him is the totally worst idea ever. You tried it once; it didn't work. That's got to be the end of it."

She was right, but she was also wrong.

And then I had an idea and realized I had to end the conversation. I let out a big sigh and said, "I guess you're right."

"I am?" Roman sounded surprised.

"Uh-huh."

"You're not just saying that to blow me off?" she asked suspiciously.

"No, it's just so frustrating," I said, pretending I wasn't completely eager to get off the phone. "You know how it feels when you want to do something and there's nothing you can do."

Roman assured me that things would work out sooner or later, then asked what my plans were for the rest of the day.

"Catch up on schoolwork," I lied. "It's really been hard to focus, and I'm way behind."

As soon as I got off with Roman, I called Whit.

"Hey." He sounded surprised to hear from me.

"I have an idea," I said. "An angle we should pursue."

"We?"

"Look, if you really want to get to the truth, you're going to need me. I know these people. I—"

"Stop," he said. "Not on the phone. I'm not saying it's tapped or anything. I just don't like taking chances."

"But we're not talking about anything people don't already know about."

There was a pause, then Whit said, "Maybe *you're* not."

Was I imagining it, or was there something about the way he said that that meant he did know something he didn't want anyone else to know about?

"When can you meet?" I asked.

"It'll have to be soon. I have to get together with a friend later."

We agreed to meet at a McDonald's halfway between Sarah Lawrence and Soundview. As I threw on some clothes, I found myself wondering who Whit's friend was. Not that I really cared. It was just curiosity. Like, what kind of friends did he have?

Downstairs, Mom was still in the kitchen, having coffee.

"Where are you going?" she asked.

"Starbucks with Roman," I said without stopping.

At McDonald's I told Whit about Gabriel and his strange attitude toward the missing girls. Whit listened quietly, but I sensed he had something else on his mind.

"That's interesting," he said when I'd finished.

"You only half listened," I said.

He raised his eyebrows, as if surprised that I'd noticed, then leaned forward and pressed the tips of his fingers together. "Can you swear to keep a secret?"

"Absolutely."

He spoke barely above a whisper. "The woman who works for your father and calls herself Janet Fontana is not Janet Fontana."

I stared at him, not sure I understood.

"Janet Fontana was a bookkeeper for a plumbing supply company in Salem, Oregon. She died in a car accident about two years ago, just a month or two after her twin sister, Jane, was released from a California prison where she'd served eighteen months for an Internet scam involving credit card fraud. It appears that when Janet's death certificate was issued, Jane doctored it to remove the *t* so it looked like Jane, not Janet, died."

"You're saying that Jane took over her sister Janet's identity?" I guessed.

"Exactly. The two sisters looked similar enough, and Jane could easily use Janet's driver's license. She moved across the country to Soundview and used her sister's IDs and the money in her Salem bank account to open a new account here, get credit cards, rent an apartment, the whole works."

It took a moment to absorb the news. Then I said, "What about the police?"

"Unlike her sister, Janet Fontana was a law-abiding citizen. I assume the police here asked the police in Salem to run a records check and it came up clean. No criminal record. Nothing that would cause the police to want to investigate any further."

"So when Jane applied for the job as Dad's office manager, she used her sister Janet's résumé," I concluded.

"Uh-huh." Whit nodded.

That explained how someone so disorganized could be hired to be an office manager.

"How . . . did you find this out?" I asked.

"The Internet," Whit said. "I was digging around and came up with an obit from the Salem *Statesman Journal* for Janet Fontana. I made a few phone calls, and when someone told me that Janet had a twin sister named Jane, who'd come to town for a few days after Janet died, I began to put the story together. Pretty simple, actually. It just took a lot of time and searching."

He paused and waited for me to digest the news. Then he said, "By the way, you might be interested to know that Mr. Kissy Face was once arrested for shooting a BB gun at a neighbor's window."

"You also found that on the Internet?" I guessed.

Whit nodded.

"So what else do you know about Janet? I mean, Jane?"

"She has a pretty long California police record. It started with small-time stuff like shoplifting and petty theft, but then she grad-uated to more serious crimes. . . . Internet scams. Felonies. That's why she did jail time."

In my mind I pictured Janet/Jane, and how scattered and moody and temperamental she could sometimes be.

"Did your dad ever say anything?" Whit asked.

"Never. Why would he hire someone like that if he knew?"

Whit tapped a finger against his head as if to say, "Think about it."

To help him with the modeling scam . . .

"Oh God," I moaned miserably.

"But that's *only* if he *knew* who she really was," Whit stressed. "Any idea how long she's been working for him?"

"A couple of years at least."

Whit unfolded a piece of paper with a column of print on it. I watched his eyes scan down, then stop. His forehead furrowed. "Could you be a little more precise?"

Strangely, I could. "Two years . . . three months . . . four days."

Whit cocked his head curiously.

"It was the week I turned sixteen. I wanted him to take me to get my driver's permit, but he couldn't leave the studio early because he had to break in the new office manager. I wanted to kill her. . . . I mean, in a manner of speaking."

"Why couldn't your mom take you?"

"She was helping him at the studio. He'd just moved it from the city. There was tons to do."

"Just curious, why'd your dad decide to move his studio up here from New York?" Whit asked.

That was a good question, and I wasn't sure I knew the answer. It had happened very quickly, and I'd always assumed that he felt he could do just as well in Soundview, but without the commute. But when he'd been in the city, there'd been lots of work and he'd never had to resort to shooting menus.

"I don't really know," I said.

Whit scowled and looked at the paper. The lines in his forehead deepened. "You sure about that date?"

"Totally. I was so PO'd about not being able to get my learner's permit until the weekend."

"So Janet had only been living here in Soundview a few weeks when she got hired," Whit said.

"I'm sure Dad didn't know who she really was," I said. The alternative was far too upsetting to consider. If Dad knew who she really was, then once again he'd lied to me. He'd said he'd fallen into the scam gradually and by accident. But if he'd *knowingly* hired Janet, that implied he'd known exactly what he was doing from the start.

Then I thought of something else. "But why would that make Janet a suspect? Isn't it a stretch to go from Internet scams to murder? And what would her motive be for killing the girls?"

"Think about it. She was living here under a false identity. She knew that if the girls complained to the police about the scam, she might get caught. And with her record, if she got caught for identity theft, she'd be going straight back to prison."

I thought back to the day the police first came to Dad's studio and how agitated Jane/Janet had been.

"But there were so many girls who fell for the scam," I said. "How does killing just three keep her out of prison?"

"Maybe they were the only ones who threatened to go to the police after they realized they'd been scammed. I mean, you've probably got some girls who didn't even realize it was a scam, and some girls who figured it out and just shrugged their shoulders and moved on. But there had to be a few who got mad and demanded their money back, or threatened to turn your dad in."

"And those would be the ones Janet was concerned about," I said. The muscles in the sides of my head began to tighten and throb. Had Whit really figured out who the killer was? If it wasn't my father, I should have felt elated, right? But if he'd knowingly wanted Janet to help in the scam, then wasn't he indirectly responsible for what happened to those girls? I felt torn with mixed emotions. And there was one more question: "So why haven't you written a story about it?"

Whit gazed at me with his steady green eyes. "I'm going to. But I'd feel a lot better if I knew what your dad knew and when he knew it. Because once this story gets out, everyone's going to think that he hired her precisely because she has experience with scams. If that's true, then the public has a right to know. But if it's not true, I'd like to be able to say so. . . ."

"Because you don't want him to be unjustly accused?" I asked.

Whit nodded, and I had to appreciate him for that, because any other journalist would probably have run the story immediately. It was a good scoop and would undoubtedly bring glory to whoever wrote about it first.

"Any ideas?" he asked.

"The answer could be somewhere in the studio," I said.

"But the police have already been there twice. They must have seen all kinds of papers and records."

Whit had been honest with me, and now I was going to be honest with him. "Yes, but both times, they were in the office . . . Janet's office."

He gave me an uncertain look.

"Dad has his own files. He keeps them in his photo studio. If the police haven't found Janet's fake résumé yet, then it might be there. It's the only way I can think of to prove that Dad hired her without knowing about her criminal background. . . . How long are you willing to hold off on publishing this story?"

His forehead wrinkled. "It's hard to wait, Shelby. I feel like at any moment someone else is going to figure out what's going on."

"Would you wait until tonight?" I asked.

He gazed back at me. "Only if you let me go with you."

chapter 24

THAT EVENING I slipped on a light jacket. "Going out, Mom," I called, then went out the door.

I'd just gotten to my car when I heard, "Shels?" Her silhouette was in the doorway. "Where are you going?"

"Just out." I immediately regretted that I hadn't been more specific. It sounded made up and feeble.

"Out where?"

"To Roman's. I won't stay late."

Mom was quiet. I couldn't see her expression. She closed the door.

Whit was waiting for me in the dark parking lot behind the studio, with two small flashlights. He gave me one. "You have the keys?" he asked.

I nodded, and we walked toward the back door. "Doesn't it feel like we're in a movie?" I whispered.

"All we're doing is going into your dad's studio."

"At night with flashlights?"

I was just about to slide the key into the back-door lock when I noticed a flat piece of plastic stuck in the doorjamb. The kind of plastic that milk containers are made out of. Someone had put it there to keep the door from locking.

I stiffened and whispered to Whit: "Think someone's in there?"

He reached past me and slowly pushed open the door. "Let me go first."

I followed him inside, my nerves tingling and heart rattling. The building was quiet and dark, and we flicked on our flashlights. As we made our way slowly down the hall toward the photo studio, Whit whispered, "Usually, when someone puts something like that in a door, it means they've left and want to be able to get back in later. So let's make sure we keep our ears open in case they come back."

Still, he shone his flashlight into the kitchenette, the broom closet, even the bathroom, just to be sure. If anyone had been there, they'd gone.

We went into the photo studio, and I swung my flashlight at the cabinets lining the wall.

Thump!

The unexpected sound came from behind me. I spun around just as Whit collapsed to the floor . . . and a dark figure sprinted out of the studio.

chapter 25

"WHIT!" I KNELT beside him. He was sprawled on the floor, his eyes squeezed shut and a grimace of intense pain on his face. His hand went to the back of his head and he moaned. "Aw, jeez . . ."

He tried to look at his hand in the dark. I shone my flashlight on it. There was no blood. Next I aimed the flashlight through the doorway to see if the person who'd hit him was still there.

But he—or she—was gone. I turned back to Whit, who'd propped himself up on one elbow. "Are you okay?"

"I guess." He pushed himself up to a sitting position, touched the back of his head again, and winced. "Ow! Man, that hurts. You sure I'm not bleeding?"

I looked at the back of his head. A bump was already starting to bulge. "Is it bad?"

"Worse than you'd imagine from watching TV."

"Whoever it was must have been hiding behind the door."

"Male or female?"

"I couldn't tell. It happened too fast."

Whit touched the back of his head again. "You wouldn't have any ice, would you?"

"Yes. Be right back." I went down to the kitchenette and put some ice in a plastic bag. When I got back to the photo studio, Whit was aiming his flashlight at the cabinets. I gave him the bag, which he pressed gently against his head.

"Thanks," he said. "Guess we better start looking."

That caught me by surprise. "You sure?"

"Yeah. Believe me, it's not the first time I've had my bell rung."

"Football?"

"Low doorways. I'm always banging my head." He slowly pushed himself up to his feet.

"Shouldn't we do something about what just happened? I mean, call the police or something?"

"And say what? That we were breaking in and I got beaned by the person who'd broken in ahead of us?"

"We didn't break in," I said. "I have a key."

"And when they ask what we were doing here in the middle of the night?" he asked, crossing to the first file cabinet.

I didn't have an answer for that.

"Whoever it was is gone," Whit said as he pulled open a cabinet and shone his flashlight inside. "All we'd be doing is drawing attention to ourselves. I'm supposed to be writing stories, not making myself the subject of them."

The cabinet was filled with light reflectors, filters, and

colored gels—but no files. We started to look in other cabinets, but they were also filled with photographic equipment.

"What made you think your dad kept files in here?" Whit asked.

"I've seen them," I said, swinging the flashlight around the studio.

"Maybe he brought them in from the office," Whit said.

"I don't think so," I said. My flashlight beam swept the walls and stopped on two large storage cabinets mounted high up. We found a ladder, and I climbed up and looked. At first it appeared that the cabinets were filled with backdrops and rolls of colored paper. I was about to give up when something told me to shove things out of the way and see what was behind them.

Bingo! In the back of the cabinets were cardboard boxes. When I opened one, I found files inside it. There were half a dozen boxes, and I started handing them down to Whit.

A few moments later we were sitting on the studio floor, reading files with our flashlights. Unlike the disorganized mess in the office, these files were orderly. The first three boxes were filled with purchase orders for head shots and makeup and other fees. There were hundreds of them, almost all for jobs in small cities in a radius of about a hundred miles from Soundview—Hartford, Springfield, Albany, Binghamton, Allentown, Wilmington, Trenton, and more. All of them girls who'd placed their dreams in my father's hands.

It was disheartening. Not just because of the money Dad had taken from them, but the dreams he'd stolen and false hopes he'd perpetrated. And the dishonesty bordering on outright theft. Pulling up purchase order after purchase order, I couldn't help wondering if the whole thing hadn't been one big scam from start to finish.

My BlackBerry vibrated. It was Mom, probably calling to say there was school tomorrow and she wanted me home. I didn't answer. Hardly a minute passed before a text arrived, this time from Roman: **WRU?**

I texted back: **Cnt Tlk,** and continued looking at the files. Whit stood up. "Just gonna get some more ice," he said, and left the studio.

I finished one box and started the next, expecting to find more purchase orders. But this one contained a few dozen head shots. Why, I wondered as I pulled up photo after photo, were these head shots here instead of in the files in Janet's office with all the others? It seemed odd until I glanced at one, started to move to the next, then froze.

I went back and looked again.

Ashley Walsh . . .

"Oh my God," I muttered.

"You find something?" Whit asked as he returned holding a new bag of ice to the back of his head.

"Uh, no, something else. I mean, nothing. Not important. Sorry."

Whit scowled at me, but I started thumbing through the files again, pretending everything was fine. Meanwhile, my thoughts were churning. So it wasn't just girls who lived a hundred miles away. They could live right here in town. Besides Ashley, how many more were from Soundview High?

My BlackBerry vibrated again. It was Mom, and I knew

without answering that she wanted me home. I turned to Whit. "I have to go."

"It's okay." He turned back to the files.

"You have to go, too."

He frowned. "Why?"

"You can't be here without me."

A surprised blink. "You . . . don't trust me?"

"It's not that. It's just that if it wasn't for me, you wouldn't be here right now. I feel responsible." I girded myself for the argument I expected from him about how important it would be to my father that we keep looking for information about Jane/Janet. So I was surprised when Whit said, "Okay."

When we left, I made sure the back studio door was firmly locked. A chilly breeze swirled around the parking lot, and I hugged myself to stay warm. Whit and I faced each other in the dark.

"How's your head?" I asked.

He touched the back of his skull and winced. "Pretty tender. But it'll be okay. A couple of Tylenols, and I should be able to sleep."

I glanced at the back door. "I thought you were going to argue about having to leave."

"I was tempted, but I understand where you're coming from. It's your dad's place, and you don't want strangers going through his things."

I felt a scowl cross my face. Whit saw it and asked, "What?"

"It's funny. I mean, I hardly know you, but you don't feel like a stranger."

He tilted his head curiously, but in the dark, it was difficult to read his expression. Even more puzzling to me was why I felt that way.

Suddenly, a pair of headlights swung into the parking lot.

Whit and I were illuminated.

And blinded.

Our only escape route blocked.

chapter 26

THE CAR'S DOOR swung open, and someone got out. Still blinded by the headlights, I couldn't see who it was. My heart thudded hard in my chest.

"Hey." The voice was friendly and unexpectedly familiar.

"Romy?" I shielded my eyes against the glare and felt light-headed with relief. "Turn off the lights. You're blinding us."

"Oh, sorry." She reached into the car and cut the headlights.

It took a moment to readjust to the dark. "What are you doing here?"

"Your mother called," Roman said. "You told her you were going to my house, so I didn't know what to say, and then she pretty much knew anyway that you weren't there."

There was something odd about the way she was speaking and how she kept glancing at Whit.

"So . . . you decided to come look for me?" I asked.

"First I texted you, but you texted back you couldn't talk, and then I got worried that maybe you were in some kind of trouble."

"How did you know I was here?" I asked.

"Just a lucky guess. Like, where else would you be?" Roman said.

I found that hard to believe. Meanwhile, she kept glancing at Whit, so I introduced them.

"I've read your stories in the *Snoop*," Roman said. "They're really good."

Whit thanked her, and she turned to me again. "So what's going on? What're you doing here?"

I didn't know how to answer. Besides, I'd just realized something. There was one sure way she could have known Whit and I were here—if she'd been here first. Had she been the one who'd slid the plastic into the doorjamb, hit Whit over the head, and run out? What better way to divert suspicion than to return and act like she didn't know what was going on?

Or had she been looking for something in the office and now come back to see if we'd found it?

Or was I just being completely over-the-top paranoid? After all, she was my best friend.

Roman was still waiting for an answer when Whit spoke up. "I asked her to bring me here. After writing all these stories about her dad, I really wanted to see the place."

"Uh-huh." From the way Roman nodded, I knew she didn't believe that. But maybe it didn't matter.

"I better get going before my mom sends the police to find me," I said.

I got into my car feeling wound up and tense about Roman

being there and about going home and facing Mom, who would demand to know why I'd lied to her and where I'd really been. I'd barely gotten out of the studio parking lot before my BlackBerry rang. It was Roman, calling from her car.

"What was that about?" she asked.

"How did you know we were there?" I asked back.

"I asked my question first," she said.

At that point I didn't care who'd asked first. I was feeling seriously stressed and suspicious. Roman was my best friend. If I couldn't trust her, then who could I trust? "I'm serious. How did you know?"

"I told you, it was a lucky guess, pure and simple. Where else would you have been?"

"I can think of a hundred places."

"Well, I don't have your imagination. So what's the story?"

"Why do you want to know?"

"I thought we were best friends," she said.

"And you've never kept a secret from me?"

"What's that got to do . . . ," she began to ask, then realized. "Oh, so *that's* the deal? I must have kept secrets from you, so it's okay for you to keep this secret from me?"

I didn't answer.

"Since when don't we trust each other?" she asked.

Was she right? Was I being crazy paranoid? She couldn't possibly have anything to do with those missing girls, could she? And yet, I still didn't understand how she could have known that Whit and I were at the studio just now. Could it really have been as simple as a lucky guess?

"I'm almost home," I lied. "I have to go in and face Mom. We'll talk about this later."

A few moments later I pulled into the driveway but didn't get out right away. I was scared. I wished I could tell Mom the truth, but Whit had made me swear that I'd keep the Janet thing a secret.

I couldn't sit in the car forever, putting off the inevitable, so I took a deep breath and got out. As I walked to the front door, I expected that Mom would be waiting in the living room.

What I didn't expect was for Dad to be waiting there, too.

chapter 27

MOM WAS SITTING on the couch. Dad was in an easy chair on the other side of the coffee table. As I closed the door behind me, he lowered a copy of the newspaper. I imagined their sitting in complete silence with Dad reading the paper while they waited for me.

"I called Roman's house," Mom began.

"I know," I said. "She told me."

"So . . . ?"

"I . . . was with a guy."

From the surprise on their faces, I knew immediately that my answer had worked.

"Really?" Dad's eyebrows rose with interest. "Someone from school?"

"He goes to Sarah Lawrence," I said.

Mom's eyebrows dipped uncertainly. "How did you meet him?"

"The day I went for my interview."

"No kidding?" Dad seemed happy for me. *How could this*

be the same man who stole from all those girls? I wondered.

It wasn't in my nature to spin lies, but I knew that Mom would want to know more. "I asked him for directions . . . and he offered to show me the way and we started to talk."

"Like an instant attraction?" Dad smiled brightly. Despite all the horrible things going on in his life, you could see that he still got a kick out of hearing how his daughter met a guy.

"Was this the first time you've seen him since then?" Mom asked.

"Oh no, I . . . we've seen each other a couple of times and talked a lot on the phone." It was interesting how, except for the part about asking for directions, almost every answer I'd given had basically been true, and how easily the true answers had fit the questions.

But then Mom said, "And suddenly tonight you just *had* to see him?"

I felt my insides tighten. How would I answer *that*?

"Oh, come on, Ruth," Dad said. "It's young love. It's passionate and impatient and impetuous."

Mom's eyes remained fixed on me as if she hadn't heard a word he'd said.

"Do we get to meet him?" Dad asked.

"Uh. . ." I hesitated. Ironically, it was Dad who'd innocently asked the question that was hardest to answer. "Maybe someday. I mean, we're not there yet, you know?"

Dad nodded and smiled. Mom just gazed silently at me as if trying to see through to the truth.

"Well, then, all right." Dad stood up as if the matter had been settled. "I think we've gotten to the bottom of that. When you're ready, Shels, I'd like to meet him." He gave Mom a terse nod and left the living room.

Mom remained on the couch, waiting, it seemed to me, until Dad was out of earshot. Then, in a low voice, she said, "I read an interesting article once. It said that everyone believes that liars aren't able to look you in the eye, so some liars go out of their way to look you in the eye to make you think they're telling the truth."

I kept my eyes on hers. Mom studied me silently. "You must stay out of this, Shelby. It's dangerous. The girl they found in that cave near Scranton didn't wind up there by accident. I know you want to protect your father, but you can't do that without putting yourself at risk."

Suddenly, I couldn't meet her gaze anymore and stared down at the floor.

"Tell me you'll stay out of it," Mom said.

"I . . . will."

"Promise me?" she said, getting up and coming toward me.

I looked up. "I said I will."

Mom kissed me on the forehead, then nodded as if to say I could go. I went upstairs and slumped down in front of my computer. The memory of how I'd left things with Roman returned. I'd been unreasonably mistrustful and must have hurt her feelings. I was wondering if I should call and apologize when a text showed up. . . from Gabriel: **Thx 4 inviting me 2 the party. W2 meet again? 121?**

That caught me by surprise. I could only assume that the quick kiss I'd given him after the party, before we'd parted, had smoothed out the earlier rough spots. It was flattering to think that he still liked me, but then I thought about the warnings both Whit and Roman had given me about him. I was wondering about how to answer him when an e-mail popped up from vengeance13772388@gmail.com: **I like you, Shelby Sloan. If I have to kill you, I'll kill you last.**

chapter 28

I ALMOST CRIED out. My hands gripped the edge of the desk, and my heart thudded heavily in my chest as I stared at the ominous words, reading them over and over.

Someone was actually threatening to kill me.

It took a while to begin to calm down and breathe normally again. *They're just words,* I told myself. *It could even be someone playing a sick joke. Besides, as long as I'm in my house, in my room, I'm safe.*

I began to think about what the words meant. The person who sent the e-mail said he liked me. Could it really be someone I knew *that* well?

And what did "If I have to kill you" mean? Why would anyone *have* to kill me? It didn't make sense . . . unless it was a warning. . . . That he would have to kill me if I didn't stop looking into my father's situation . . .

But why send the e-mail now? Why hadn't he sent it a few days ago? And didn't it imply that I was onto something? Clearly, whoever sent it did so because he was feeling threatened by me.

So who knew that I was looking into Dad's case? Whit and Roman . . . and the person who'd hit Whit on the head tonight.

I felt frightened, but also, strangely, encouraged. I must have been getting closer to the answer. But now what? The thought of telling my parents came and quickly passed. Telling Dad about the e-mail would make him freak out, and telling Mom would only confirm what she'd just finished saying in the living room—that if I continued to snoop around, I was in danger of becoming a target myself. It would become a great big "I told you so" moment for her and would probably result in my being completely grounded.

So forget that.

Besides, there had to be ways to proceed carefully. From now on when I went out at night, I would make sure to be with someone. And if I needed to investigate something, I would ask Whit along.

Whit . . . It was interesting how useful he'd become, both in my "investigation" and as an alibi. Why did I feel I could trust him when it felt so hard to trust anyone else? Didn't he have the most to gain from ingratiating himself to me? How did I know for sure that he wasn't using me? Pretending to be my friend and searching for *the truth* until he got the really *big* story? The one that would guarantee him the job in journalism that he so dearly wanted? Since when had I become such a great judge of character that I knew everyone's motives?

And, if he *was* using me to get that story, wasn't it possible that *he'd* sent that threatening e-mail? What better way to ensure that

I'd keep him involved in the investigation than to make me feel like I needed him for protection?

But if I couldn't trust him, then who could I trust?

Or, had I reached the point . . . where I couldn't trust anyone?

I made sure the windows in my room were locked. Then I locked my door and wedged a chair under the doorknob. And still lay awake in the dark for a long time.

They reported on TV the next morning that the body found in the cave near Scranton had been positively identified as Rebecca Parlin. The report said that it would still be some time before the police would be able to pinpoint the cause of death.

I knew I shouldn't have been surprised, but it was still a blow. Yet another step closer to a horrible ending.

And now there was school, which I wasn't looking forward to attending. Not only because all those kids would once again be staring, as if they thought Dad was the murderer, but because I'd have to face Roman, knowing that we'd argued and that I'd implied that I was no longer sure I could trust her.

I decided to get to lunch early. That way when Roman got to the cafeteria, I'd already be at our regular table and it would be up to *her* to decide whether to sit with me. As soon as the bell rang, I was out of my seat and racing toward the cafeteria. Usually the only ones who hurried to lunch were hungry guys, and luckily I found myself behind Dave Curlin, a football player who charged through the crowded hallway as if trying to score a touchdown.

In the cafeteria, I was relieved to see that Roman's and my table was empty. But as I headed toward it, I became aware that someone else was also getting closer. It was Roman, hurrying in from the other side of the cafeteria. We reached the table at the same time and stood across from each other, each knowing exactly why the other had been in a rush.

Then we both sat.

Roman was the first to speak: "See the news this morning?"

"Uh-huh."

"No surprise, I guess."

"Uh-huh." I made no effort to hide my reluctance to talk.

Roman studied me. "Why are you acting like this?"

"I still don't understand how you could have known where I was last night."

"I told you, it was just a lucky guess," she insisted.

It was obvious that no matter how many times I asked, she was going to give the same answer.

"So . . . when did you and Whit get together?" she asked.

I felt myself relax a little. We were back in familiar territory — talking about guys. Of course, I couldn't tell her the news about Janet/Jane's identity theft and criminal record, but I could be vague. "I guess we're both interested in the same thing."

"So you've gotten him to help you try to figure out what's going on?" Roman shot me a knowing smile. "Or is that just the excuse you're using to spend time with him?"

"He's not my type."

"What's wrong with big and blond?"

"Did you see his nose?"

Roman shook her head. "It was dark. Why? Something wrong with it?"

"It's crooked. Like that actor's? I can't remember if he said how he broke it."

"I thought things like that give you character," she said.

Whit had character, but I wasn't sure it had anything to do with his nose. Personality-wise, he seemed like a solid, dependable, serious guy. But physically, he was big, ponderous, and, though gentle, also clumsy. Sexy, he wasn't.

"He reminds me of Lennie in *Of Mice and Men*," I said. "I mean, not the dumb part; he's actually really smart. But there's something about him that just doesn't work for me."

As we started to eat, Tara Kraus and her posse entered the cafeteria. And there was Ashley. In all the drama of the night before—Whit being hit on the head, Roman showing up at the studio, the life-threatening e-mail from vengeance—I'd forgotten what I'd discovered in the cabinet in Dad's studio.

"Be right back." As I started across the lunchroom, Tara and a few others turned to look, but Ashley didn't. Still, I could tell that she'd seen me out of the corner of her eye because her stride stiffened and she stared straight ahead.

In the middle of the cafeteria, surrounded by tables filled with chattering kids, Tara stopped to face me. If she'd been a porcupine, her bristles would have been in full bloom. The girls around her glowered, but Ashley seemed to shrink down behind them.

"Ashley," I said.

"What do you want?" Tara's nostrils flared. I wondered if she'd start snorting and pawing the floor next.

I ignored her and looked directly at Ashley. "Can we talk?"

An anxious scowl crossed my old friend's face. "Why?"

"I have to ask you something . . . in private."

"You don't have to talk to her," Tara said.

Ashley's eyes darted at Tara, then back at me. She tilted her head at the windows, as if we should go over there.

"Want me to come?" Tara asked.

Ashley shook her head.

We walked toward the windows. Outside, orange and white koi glided gracefully through the dark water of the small pond the PTO had built in the center of the courtyard. Ashley bit the corner of her lip.

"I didn't know you'd signed up with my dad's agency," I said.

She nodded and let her breath out in a way that made me think that wasn't what she'd expected me to say.

"I guess I was surprised because we used to be friends and we still see each other almost every day at school," I said.

She gave me a quick glance. "So I was supposed to tell you?"

In a way, she was right. It wasn't mandatory for me to know. There wasn't a rule. It just felt strange. "Did anything ever happen?" I asked.

"What do you mean?"

"Did he get you any modeling jobs?"

Her brow dipped with consternation. "If I'd gotten modeling jobs, you think I'd still be working at Playland?"

She was right. "I'm sorry, that was a stupid question. But did he at least send you to some tryouts?"

"A few, but nothing ever came out of them."

Her answer was enough to make me feel relieved. So at least as far as Ashley was concerned, it hadn't been a scam. Dad had tried to get her some work.

Ashley crossed her arms tightly and glanced back at the lunch line, as if she was eager to go. "That's all you wanted to know?"

"Yes," I said.

"Well, okay, great. See ya." She started back across the cafeteria.

As I watched her go, I thought about her last question. *Was that all I wanted to know?*

That's when I realized I'd asked the wrong questions.

chapter 29

I WAS IN the library last period when I got a text from Gabriel: **C my txt last nite?**

I'd totally forgotten. The previous night, his text had come just a moment before the e-mail threatening to kill me. No wonder I'd lost track. Now I texted back: **Yes. Sorry. TTLY distracted.**

Gabriel: **C U After schl?**

Once again the memory of the party came back. How frustrated he'd gotten when I hadn't been willing to go somewhere alone with him. And how I'd felt bad about misleading him and had given him that kiss.

Roman and Whit had both warned me that he might be dangerous. But they'd never spent any real time with him. While he did seem narcissistic and lacking in empathy, he didn't strike me as particularly threatening. Besides, it wasn't like I could invite either of them along if I agreed to meet him.

And there was still a chance he might know something that would help me prove Dad's innocence. So I texted: **OK.**

He wrote: **PUUP?**

No, I thought. I might not have believed he was dangerous, but I'd told myself not to take any chances with anyone, and that included getting in his car or going anywhere alone with him.

I wrote: **Meet SMWHR?**

He wrote: **WHR?**

It was nice out, so I suggested the park near the Sound. On a day like today, it would be filled with people.

We agreed to meet at the wooden gazebo on the rocks by the water's edge. When I got there, Gabriel was sitting on a bench. He gave me a friendly smile. "Hey, how's it going?"

"Okay, I guess." I sat down beside him. The sun warmed my face. Its rays glinted off the water. Sailboats rocked at their moorings. "I mean, not great. You heard the news about that girl this morning, right?"

Gabriel nodded. "Terrible."

I was relieved to hear him say that. Maybe he wasn't so self-absorbed after all. Maybe all that glancing at his reflection was just insecurity. You had to give people the benefit of the doubt. Especially when they were as gorgeous as Gabriel.

"It's hard to believe," he went on. "These girls signed with us, and now they're turning up dead?"

"Just one," I reminded him.

He slid his eyes at me, as if to ask if I really believed the other two girls hadn't met the same fate.

"I know," I admitted. "You have to think that whatever happened to her happened to the others. I'm just praying I'm wrong."

"And maybe it's still all some kind of incredibly weird coincidence," he said. "Like maybe it has nothing to do with their being your dad's clients. Maybe there's something else that links those girls that no one's even thought of yet. The problem is, nobody knows. And nobody's *going* to know until they know, you know?"

I felt a slight and unexpected smile grow on my lips.

"What is it?" he asked.

"Nothing. I completely agree. It's just all those *knows*, you know?"

He shot me a self-deprecating grin and said sheepishly, "Welcome to my huge fifty-word vocabulary."

I chuckled, once again glad he'd asked me to meet him. It was a relief to see his charming side.

A seagull landed on the rocks and cocked its head as it studied us with one eye.

"Take a walk?" Gabriel suggested.

"Sure."

We started on a path along the shore. Ahead was a low brick structure—the bathhouse of the small beach club for town residents open from Memorial Day to Labor Day. Now that the season was over, town workers were preparing it for the winter. From the cans and drop cloths piled near the entrance, it appeared that they were giving the inside a fresh coat of paint.

Gabriel craned his neck through the open front doorway. "What's in there?"

"Lockers and changing rooms families rent over the summer."

"I want to see." He took my hand and led me inside. My hand

in his felt very natural, as if he needed my assurance while he explored this new place. But at the same time, like anyone else in my position, I was acutely aware of the possibilities. Would he try to kiss me next? Did I want him to?

We walked down a corridor bordered by freshly painted lockers, the smell of drying paint in our noses. Just as we passed the ladies' room, I felt Gabriel's hand tighten. He stopped and turned me toward him, pulling me close.

We were alone.

I felt his arms go around me.

I closed my eyes.

chapter 30

HIS EMBRACE TIGHTENED.

Then tightened more.

Suddenly, I felt myself being lifted off my feet, my arms pinned at my sides. Alarm spreading, I opened my eyes and tried to squirm out of his grasp, but his grip was too tight and too close for me to get any leverage.

"Gabriel, stop! What are you doing?" I gasped when I realized he was dragging me into the ladies' room. He swung the door closed behind us, then pushed me hard against the walls.

When my eyes focused, I was staring at a knife.

The blade was curved and sharp on one edge and serrated on the other. I stopped breathing and felt as if my heart was trying to crawl into my throat. Gabriel held the knife just below my neck.

"Don't move; don't yell," he whispered.

I'm not sure I could have done either, even if he'd ordered me to. I was frozen with fear.

"Don't do anything dumb, and you won't get hurt," he growled.

I didn't move. I didn't speak. My heart thumped so hard I could feel the pulse throbbing in my neck. *Breathe*, I told myself. *If you stop breathing, you'll faint.* But I was beginning to feel sick and light-headed with fear. So it was Gabriel? He was the killer?

"I need money," Gabriel said.

I heard him clearly, but was so surprised that I almost asked him to repeat it. Money? "I think I have thirty dollars."

"No, stupid!" he snapped. "*Real* money. Fifty thousand."

What? "I don't—"

"Your father has it."

My father? Fifty thousand dollars?

"He's been avoiding me. Won't go into the same room, won't answer the phone. I made him so frickin' much money, and now it's like I don't exist."

I was trying to understand, but my brain was sluggish with fright. The knife looked new and sharp, and it was so close to my neck. "How?"

"How what?"

"Did you—"

"Make him so much money?" Gabriel finished the sentence. "I was the cheese in the mouse trap. Janet would talk the pigeons in, and then I would soften them up for the kill."

Mice? Pigeons? Was it advisable to tell someone holding a knife to your throat that he was mixing metaphors?

"The kill?" I repeated.

"We didn't *kill* anyone," Gabriel growled. "That's just what we called it. Janet got them to come to the hotel, but once they were there, it was my job to romance them, make them feel beautiful enough to think they could be models, make their mothers feel beautiful enough to think their daughters could do it. I was the closer, the charmer, the one who got the mothers to part with the money. Without me the whole thing wouldn't have worked."

"But Dad paid you, didn't he?"

Gabriel snorted. "Nothing compared to what he kept for himself. And now I need more, and he's got it, and you're going to get him to give it to me."

That's when it dawned on me. *I was being kidnapped? Held for ransom?*

"He's got till the end of the week, or I go to the police."

It didn't make sense. This person holding a knife on me was threatening to go to the police? Shouldn't I have been the one who threatened to do that?

"You got it?" Gabriel lowered the knife, which was a huge relief.

"No, I don't understand. The police have already questioned him. They know about the scam."

Gabriel smirked. "They don't know anything."

"Then tell me."

He shook his head. "Just tell him he's got till the end of the week. He'll know what I'm talking about." He stepped back, slid the knife into his pocket, and gazed at me. "Too bad it had to go this way. You and I could have had a nice thing together."

I thought of pinching myself to make sure this wasn't a dream. This guy pulls a knife on me and then talks about what a cute couple we might have been? Was one of us in serious need of a reality check? But I held my tongue. He still had that knife.

"Get out of here," he said.

I started to back out of the ladies' room. As Gabriel watched, a nasty curl appeared on his lips. "Oh, wait, there's something I always meant to tell you. You know all those photographs of famous people your dad has hanging on his walls? They're stock shots he bought on eBay."

"But they're autographed to him."

Gabriel chuckled. "Not autographed *to* him, autographed *by* him. They're fakes. Now go. And remember, one word to anyone, and your dad is toast."

I backed through the door, not taking my eyes off him until I was in the hallway, where I could turn and run. Outside the bathhouse, I started to walk quickly, wondering if I should go to the police anyway. What if Gabriel was bluffing? Hoping I'd believe him and not get the police involved?

But what if he *wasn't* bluffing?

Was it possible that Dad had been up to even worse than what I already knew?

chapter 31

I GOT HOME in time to find a handful of photographers shooting pictures of a Soundview Police Department wrecker towing Dad's Ferrari out of the driveway. I hurried to the front door. Dad was sitting in the kitchen with a bowl of peanuts, a bottle of tequila, and a shot glass. Dark stubble lined his jaw, his hair was disheveled, his shirt hung out.

"You know what they're doing?" I tilted my head in the direction of the driveway.

He nodded slowly, almost hopelessly.

I sat down at the table with him. "Dad, brace yourself." When I told him what had just happened with Gabriel, Dad's bloodshot eyes widened with fury. He placed his hands on the table and lurched up unsteadily. The chair he'd been sitting on clattered backward and banged into the kitchen counter. He staggered a step or two toward the kitchen door and shoved his hand into his pocket as if to take out his car keys, then stopped and cursed loudly, as if he'd just remembered that his car was no longer there. In frustration, he spun around and kicked the chair across the kitchen.

"What's going on?" Mom gasped, appearing in the doorway.

"When I get my hands on that punk, I'll . . ." Dad grumbled and staggered again, turning his head this way and that, as if uncertain which direction to go.

"What's wrong?" Mom asked.

Dad and I looked at each other with, I was convinced, the same thought—was this something we wanted her to know about? Unfortunately, we were a little too obvious about it.

"You're not going to tell me?" Mom's voice was filled with helpless disappointment.

Dad nodded at me, as if giving his approval. I told her what had happened.

By the time I'd finished, Mom was reaching for the phone. "We have to call the police."

"Don't," Dad said.

She stared at him. "Why not?"

Dad took a deep breath, picked up the chair, and sat down, letting out a trembling, almost defeated sigh. "Just . . . don't."

"But we're talking about someone who threatened our daughter with a knife," Mom said, taking the phone off the hook.

Dad glanced at me and then said, "You can't call them, Ruth. You know why."

From the way Mom reacted, I wasn't sure she did. But she must have figured it out pretty fast. Looking shaken, she slowly replaced the phone on the hook.

At the table, Dad knocked back the rest of the tequila in his glass, his shoulders stooped with defeat. The kitchen became quiet and filled with a heavy sense of gloom.

"Is someone going to tell me why Mom can't call the police?" I asked.

Mom looked at Dad, then at me. "Oh, darling, I really don't think you need to—"

"I—" Dad began, and Mom instantly quieted. He rubbed his hand across his forehead and stared at the table. "I don't . . . want the police to know . . . because . . ." He leaned forward and pressed his face into his hands. For a moment I wondered if he was going to break down.

Mom stared at me, her eyes filling with tears, then turned to him. "You don't have to tell her."

He lowered his hands and stared at the table. "Some of the things you've heard . . . are true, Shels."

A tremor ran through me. "You . . . had something to do with the missing girls?"

"No, not that, but . . . I . . . took advantage."

For a moment the words didn't compute . . . then they did. Mom turned and looked out the window so I couldn't see her face.

"What about . . . the ones who are missing?" I asked.

Dad nodded.

I stood there stunned. Numb. Thinking back to what the girl on TV said about Dad wanting to meet her alone. *My own father* . . . I thought.

Mom hurried out of the kitchen. Her footsteps raced up the stairs, and a door slammed.

Dad hadn't moved. He was still staring at the table. "They said . . . they were all over eighteen."

Again it took a moment for me to understand. *Over eighteen?* Oh God, so that, according to the law, meant they were legal? But the way he'd just said that—

"You're . . . not sure?"

He didn't answer.

"Did you hurt them?" I asked.

He shook his head.

"Are you *sure*?"

Dad winced. "You doubt me?"

I stared at him in disbelief, feeling frustration and incredulity mutate into anger. "Do I doubt you? If I do, can you blame me? Every day, you reveal something new and swear that that's the end of it. And then the next day, there's always something else and it's always worse. What's next, Dad? What horrible thing will we find out tomorrow?"

"Nothing."

"Yeah, right," I scoffed.

"I swear, Shels."

I stared at him. His gaze dropped. I remembered what Mom had said about liars keeping their eyes on yours. I thought about what Gabriel had said about those autographed photos that hung on the studio walls. *So many lies . . .*

"Please, Dad, don't swear if it's not true."

He refilled the shot glass and took a drink. "This time it's true. I swear." The kitchen became quiet again. I heard a creak from upstairs and wondered what Mom was doing. I stood with my arms crossed tightly, as if to keep myself from exploding. I wanted to understand. I wanted to come up with an "Oh, it's just Dad being Dad" explanation. But how could I understand his being with girls my age? The things he must have told them . . . *promised* them . . . to get them . . .

I shivered. It was disgusting. There was no other way to describe it. *A man his age. A man in his position of power and influence over young, naïve, starstruck girls. The old casting-couch routine, indeed,* I thought bitterly. The girls I knew would have called him a dirty old man and gross. And for good reason. And now I had to face the fact that my own father wasn't *just* one of those . . . those men who stared a little too long. He was something far, far worse.

DAD TOOK ANOTHER slug of tequila. Was he bracing himself? Did he expect an outburst from me? I was angry, and growing angrier, and tempted to say something mean, feeling like I needed to vent but trying at the same time not to. It wasn't just what he'd done to those girls. It was what he'd done to Mom and me, too. Did he ever think about us and what would happen if people found out?

It was hard to imagine anything more disappointing, or humiliating. My own father . . . was practically a child molester.

Suddenly, I couldn't stand being in the same room with him. I understood exactly how Mom felt. I ran upstairs and sat down on my bed, seething, the same question rolling over and over into my brain, as if it was coming off an assembly line: How could he?

How *could* he?

How could he?

He was despicable. I thought of the photos of those famous actors and models, and how Dad had faked them, just as he'd faked everything he'd been doing, pretending to be a successful photographer when he was really just preying on young women for money and sex. There was symbolism in thinking of our family at that moment. Mom and I upstairs in our bedrooms, the high and righteous. Dad downstairs, not exactly in a dungeon, but low and contemptible just the same. He deserved it. Unlike the other times, I couldn't even begin to try to forgive what he'd done.

I heard a soft knock on my door. "May I come in?" Dad asked.

I didn't answer. I had to think about it.

"Sweetheart?" he said after waiting.

I gritted my teeth. Had he called any of those other girls sweetheart? The thought threatened to make me ill. I waited until the sensation passed, then thought the same thing I always thought: he was still my father. "I guess."

He stopped inside the door, as if afraid to come any closer, his hands shoved into his pockets. He was a rumpled, disheveled mess, his eyes downcast. "I'm sorry. I was incredibly stupid. I made mistakes. I . . . never really thought about the consequences."

It sounded heartfelt, and despite how angry I was, I also felt sad that he'd come to me and not to Mom, as if he assumed that she was a lost cause. As if I was his only chance.

"Sweetheart?"

That word made me want to scream, but I gathered myself in. "Don't ask me for forgiveness, Dad," I said, keeping my voice flat and unemotional, "because I am so far away from that right now. . . . I just have to ask you one more time, because there've been *way* too many surprises. Just swear to me that this is the end of it. That this is as bad as it gets and it doesn't get any worse."

"It doesn't get any worse. I swear."

"Then why can't we go to the police and tell them what Gabriel did? If they're going to find out about you and those girls anyway . . ."

Dad ran his hand over his head, letting his hair flop wherever it wanted. "I don't want them to know."

"So Gabriel gets to threaten me with a knife and go free?" It was incredible.

Dad gazed at me with sad, weary, reddened eyes and didn't answer.

"And what about the money? He said he'd go to the police if he didn't get it by the end of the week."

As if lost in thought, Dad gazed off. Suddenly, I caught a glimmer of what was in his head. "You're not . . . seriously considering *paying* him, are you?"

No reply. I was shocked. I couldn't believe he would acquiesce to Gabriel's demands. "Dad, you *can't. . . .*"

"Shelby, please, don't. Not now. Give it a rest."

He sounded like he was in agony. I had to wonder if he could pay Gabriel even if he wanted to. I had no idea if my parents had any money in the bank. We had our house. And the only other things of value that Dad owned were his camera equipment and his car, which reminded me.

"Why did they take the Ferrari?"

"DNA tests. I assume they got a sample from the body

they found in Scranton and want to see if anything in my car matches it."

"Was . . . she ever in your car?" I asked.

Dad made a helpless gesture with his hands. "Who remembers?"

chapter 33

WE WERE ON overload, being bombarded by too much all at once. Gabriel's blackmail demands, the death of one girl while the other two were still missing, and all of Dad's admissions about the things he'd done wrong, each worse than the last. Under those circumstances, could any family have banded together to face their common enemies?

Not ours.

I don't know how I managed to sleep that night. The next morning before school, I checked the *Soundview Snoop* and found Whit's story about Jane/Janet's criminal history and the theft of her sister's identity. Even though we still didn't know if Dad had been aware of her past when he hired her, I was glad Whit had gone ahead with the story, if for no other reason than that it diverted some of the spotlight from my father.

The house was quiet when I left. I didn't know where Mom or Dad were. Outside, the police officer assigned to the media horde cleared a path out of the driveway, and I went to school.

For the first few periods, it felt like a normal day at school. But then, in third period English, the boy who sat next to me tapped my shoulder and gestured toward the door. Roman was out in the hall, making an urgent "I have to talk to you *now*!" face.

I got a bathroom pass and went out. Roman started talking before I even closed the classroom door: "That woman who worked for your dad? Janet? The police have taken her into custody. They say she's a person of interest, not a suspect, but who are they kidding?"

I felt a sad heaviness settle around my shoulders. It sounded like Whit's theory had come true. Jane/Janet had probably killed the girls because they'd threatened to go to the police. "And listen to this," Roman said, pulling her iPad out of her bag. "There's a story in the *New York Times* about your friend."

"What friend?" I had no idea who she was talking about.

"Lennie? From *Of Mice and Men*?"

I reached for the iPad. The story was about the rise of hyper-local Internet news sites like the *Snoop,* and it featured Whit's story about Janet as an example of how the journalism on these sites was improving. They even had a photo of Whit.

"Pretty impressive," Roman said.

"Know what's amazing?" I said. "The first time I met him, he talked about how he hoped that covering this story would get him the recognition he needed to get a good job. Like he had it all planned."

"What if *he's* the killer?" Roman asked. "He commits the crime and then covers it as a reporter. And since he knows better than anyone else who did it, he can constantly scoop everyone. And that makes him look like a media star!"

I couldn't help smiling. "Sounds like a great movie. And while you're at it, why don't you make him a vampire?"

"Be serious," she scoffed. "That's been totally overdone."

Inside the girls' room, I took out my phone.

"Texting someone?" Roman guessed.

"Uh-huh."

"Even though he reminds you of Lennie?"

"Just congratulating him." I pressed Send, then realized that Roman was giving me a funny look.

"What?" I asked.

"I just told you that the police took Janet into custody," she said. "Which suggests that they no longer think your dad is a suspect, right? So why aren't you acting like this is the best news since the invention of sliced bread?"

"Uh . . . If anything, what I'm feeling is huge relief," I said, still upset by all the other things Dad had done that Roman didn't know about.

"Did you ever think she was the culprit?"

I was about to answer when a text came back.

"That was fast," Roman said with a smile.

Whit had texted: **C U after scl?**

I felt a chilling jolt, and the breath rushed out of my lungs. It was the exact same message Gabriel had sent the day before.

chapter 34

"WHOA, DID YOU just go white?" Roman asked. "What's that about?"

"Nothing." I started to breathe again. It had to be a coincidence . . . didn't it?

"Nothing?" Roman repeated doubtfully. "For a second, I thought you were going to faint."

I shook my head and focused on trying to relax. *Just a coincidence*, I told myself again.

"I wish I knew what was going on in your head," Roman said.

"I think you'd be disappointed."

"Why don't I believe that?"

"Give me a moment." I texted Whit: **W U sneak up in prkng lot?**

Back came: **LOL. Meet @ reservoir?**

That caught me by surprise. The reservoir was in a wooded area, and the only people who went there were dog walkers and kids who wanted to drink or get high. After what happened with Gabriel, I couldn't help but feel wary: **Y thr?**

I was waiting for a text back when the phone vibrated. Whit had decided to call rather than text. I held up my finger to Roman to let her know I needed a moment, then answered. "Hey."

"Can you talk?" Whit asked.

"Barely."

"I suggested the reservoir because it's probably not a good idea for us to be seen together. Ever since the *Times* article this morning, everyone knows who I am, and obviously a lot of people around town know who you are."

I didn't get it. "We can't be seen talking?"

"It would be better . . . if my competition didn't know."

It was a jarring reminder that, as far as he was concerned, I was still a source of information. "All right," I said. "I'll see you there."

I hung up knowing Roman would give me the third degree. "He wants to talk about what's going on," I said.

"In person?"

"Yeah. At the reservoir."

Roman smiled. "Ooh la la. You're going to meet him alone?"

I rolled my eyes and headed back to class.

The reservoir was in the woods with some hiking trails and a few private homes around it. When I got to the gravel parking lot, Whit's car wasn't there. I sat and waited, listening to my iPod and watching a few yellow and orange leaves flutter down from branches.

After a while, a car pulled into the lot, but it wasn't Whit's. A blonde woman got out with a chocolate Lab, which quickly bounded off into the woods. As the woman started to follow, she glanced in my direction, as if wondering why I was sitting there in my car.

When Whit was twenty minutes late, I took out my Black-Berry to text him, but before I could push Send, he texted me: **BRT**

I closed my phone. Okay, he was coming.

Another ten minutes passed before he pulled into the lot. We both got out.

"Sorry," he said.

"Everything okay?" I asked.

"Not really. A lot's going on." He nodded at my car. "Sit in a car or take a walk?"

I couldn't help hesitating a moment. Another walk with another guy? But it was Whit, and I had to believe he wasn't carrying a knife. "It's nice out," I said. "Let's walk."

We started along the dirt path through trees with leaves beginning to turn orange and yellow.

"They found another body," he said. "This one in some woods outside Hartford."

"Peggy D'Angelo," I said, and felt my heart grow heavy.

"They haven't made a positive ID yet," Whit said. "But her hands and feet were bound like the girl near Scranton, and her description matches Peggy D'Angelo's. I guess now that they found Rebecca Parlin, they have a better idea of where to look."

More terrible news . . . I'd always known that it was hopeless to believe that the other two missing girls might still be alive, but now it seemed certain not to be the case. It was horrible and awful, and I couldn't help thinking of those girls' parents and the agony they must have been in.

"I heard they've taken Janet into custody," I said. "Was that why you were late?"

Whit shook his head. "There's something else. That other woman, Mercedes? Her family's reported her missing."

I stopped and stared at him.

"They just reported it an hour ago," he said.

I felt sick. Not Mercedes, too. Then I realized something. "If it happened an hour ago, Janet couldn't have anything to do with it. Didn't they take her into custody this morning after your story came out?"

"The family only *reported* her missing an hour ago. She could have been gone longer than that. You don't know how long they waited before calling the police."

It was too much. Tears came to my eyes. All Mercedes cared about was her little boy, Pedro. She'd never meant any harm to anyone. And yet, in an awful way, it made sense. Jane/Janet would have known that Dad and Gabriel would never go to the police because they were as guilty of the scam as she was. But she might have become concerned that if the police questioned Mercedes, she'd talk.

I wiped my eyes on my sleeve and sniffed.

Whit stared at the ground. "Hard to believe stuff like this really happens."

We went for a while without speaking. The path wound

through the trees and close to the water. A few surprised mallards quacked and swam away from shore, leaving small wakes in the dark green water. I kept thinking about Mercedes. And that made me think of the girls whose bodies had been discovered. "Have they said how Rebecca Parlin died?"

"Compressive asphyxia. In the crime world, it's called burking. They pin you to the ground on your back and press their knees down on your chest, which keeps you from breathing."

The thought of it made me wince. "Why would anyone kill someone that way?"

"Here are some guesses," Whit said. "First, there's no murder weapon involved. In any murder trial, connecting the weapon to the killer is a key piece of evidence. So the person who's doing this is making it harder for the police to connect them to the murders. Second, there are no obvious wounds, so it's conceivable that whoever's doing this could claim the deaths were accidental."

We climbed up to an old wooden bench in a small clearing and sat. I waited for him to continue, and when he didn't, I said, "Any other thoughts?"

"Well . . ." He leaned forward, resting his elbows on his knees. "It's a pretty sadistic way to kill someone. You get to be there, watching this person slowly die."

"You think the killer is a sadist?"

"Maybe someone who's either really, really angry or really, really sick. Which is why I . . ." He didn't finish.

"Why you?"

He sighed. "You know this woman, Janet?"

"A little."

"Really sick or really angry?"

I understood what he was implying. Strangely, it was a vaguely uncomfortable feeling I'd had as well. "Neither. Just flaky and disorganized and overwhelmed. Almost like the kind of person who might turn to crime simply because she couldn't function well enough to survive otherwise."

Whit nodded. We sat quietly. The mallards were now bobbing peacefully in the water.

"You've thought a lot about this," I said.

"I've tried. One thing this situation has taught me is how careful you have to be about what you think and write. Everyone's chomping at the bit to say Janet's the killer. I've even heard some of the media say it should be called a serial-killing spree. But so far only two bodies have been found. It's true they were both murdered and there seems to be a connection through your father. But I'm not sure that means Janet's the one, and even more doubtful that she fits the profile of a serial killer."

"And you think the media keeps hinting at it because it'll sell more news," I said. "Everybody's in it for their own gain."

Whit nodded. "Kind of depressing."

There was something about the way he said it that made me wonder. Like maybe some of the things he was learning about journalism weren't what he'd expected. We sat for a while longer, looking at the water and the mallards. Then Whit suggested we walk again.

"So how's it going at home?" he asked as we followed the path through the trees.

"Off the record?" I asked.

"Yes."

"Not good. My parents weren't exactly getting along to begin with. And my father can't work, so I think money's a problem." I knew better than to say anything about Gabriel and the blackmail. Or regarding Dad's admission about what he did with those girls.

But then Whit asked a question I didn't expect. "What about Mr. Kissy Face?"

Was he asking because he was curious about whether I was having a relationship with Gabriel? Strangely, I discovered I liked the idea that Whit might be interested. But then I remembered telling him about how uncomfortable I was about the oddly unempathetic way Gabriel sometimes acted. That was probably what he was referring to.

"Haven't heard from him lately. I have to assume he has his own problems."

We stopped on a wooden footbridge over a small stream. Yellow and red leaves floated on the dark water under us.

"Any job offers yet?" I asked.

He shrugged. "You mean, after being written up in the *Times*? Actually, it's been pretty quiet. And you? Any thoughts about Sarah Lawrence?"

"Haven't had time to think about it. I mean, I guess I want to go to a bigger school than that. I only went to the interview because my mom wanted me to. I don't see how we could afford it now anyway." Whit gazed away. I couldn't see his expression. "What about you?" I asked. "The last we talked about it, you weren't so gung ho about the school, either."

He looked at me with those pale green eyes. Were they merely pensive, or also a little sad?

"I think I'm going to stay there. The classes are small and the professors are great, and they do offer a pretty wide range of courses."

"But you said not that many in journalism . . ."

"No, not that many," he repeated, almost wistfully.

Did that mean he wasn't as excited about the profession as he'd been only a few days before? A light breeze blew through the trees around us, rattling the leaves. A few fell gently.

Then he said, "You might want to give Sarah Lawrence more serious consideration. Even though it's small and close by, it could be a really good place for you."

I wondered why he'd said that. We hardly even knew each other. How could he know what school would be good for me?

"You think?" I asked.

The slightest smile appeared on his lips. "Yeah, I do." He pushed himself away from the railing, and we started back toward the parking lot.

And that's when it occurred to me that maybe part of the reason he'd wanted to meet had nothing at all to do with Janet, Gabriel, Dad, or the murdered girls.

chapter 35

BACK AT HOME, Mom and Dad were in silent mode and avoiding being in the same room at the same time. I made a conscious effort to divide my time between them. But it wasn't easy. Mom was understandably distant, sullen, and uncommunicative; and while Dad tried to be affectionate and open, it was impossible for me to be with him without feeling furious about what he'd done.

And then there was the TV. Like the Sirens who tempted Odysseus in the *Odyssey*, it was both tempting and the source of great misery. We tried to keep it off as much as possible. But there were moments, usually first thing in the morning, and around dinnertime, when it was impossible to ignore.

That evening around dinnertime, hunger forced me down to the kitchen. Dad was boiling hot dogs and heating baked beans. He was clean-shaven and was wearing jeans and a freshly laundered shirt.

"Hey," he said with an unconvincing smile. "Feel like

joining me for this gastronomic extravaganza? I made a few extra dogs."

Even though I was still angry, I started to take plates out of the cupboard.

"So how was your day?" he asked.

"Okay." I didn't want to talk about Jane/Janet, or the discovery of the second body.

"How are things at school?"

"Okay."

Dad glanced at me, then nodded as if accepting the fact that I didn't want to talk. Ever since I was a little girl, I'd been warned about strangers. About what they might offer and what they really wanted. I'd been taught to be careful and watchful and suspicious. There were men who would say or do anything to get what they desired.

But whoever thinks . . . that one of them could be your own father?

When the hot dogs and beans were ready, we ate in silence. I guess Dad realized that there was nothing he could say. That whatever was going to happen next between us would be my decision. In a strange way, I appreciated him for that.

At a few minutes before six, he glanced at the kitchen clock. We both knew there would be reports on the TV about the latest developments.

"We don't have to watch," I said.

But Dad turned it on anyway. "Can't get worse. If it did, I'd know about it, right?"

On the TV, Police Chief Jenkins stood at a podium with

microphones. His forehead glistened with sweat, and he squinted in the bright TV lights. "All right. I'll read a short statement and then take some questions." He put on a pair of reading glasses. "Earlier today, at the request of the police in Hartford and Scranton, we took Jane Fontana in for questioning regarding the murdered young women from those cities. Miss Fontana is an employee of the Sloan Photographic and Modeling Agency. It is alleged that she may have committed identity theft in an attempt to hide a lengthy criminal record."

I glanced at Dad, who nodded gravely. "Until this morning I had no idea."

I could only hope that he was telling the truth.

Chief Jenkins continued: "After several hours of questioning, as well as a search of Miss Fontana's home and car, detectives uncovered evidence that appears to link her to the murders. Therefore, she is being held pending charges. Investigators are working on several possible motives in the case. That's all I have to say right now."

A barrage of questions followed. I wondered if Whit was in the crowd of reporters, but the camera stayed on the police chief. A reporter wanted to know what evidence had been found linking Janet to the two missing women. Chief Jenkins talked about traces of mud on her car that had come from the crime scenes, as well as rope that matched the rope used to tie the victims' hands and feet. Someone else asked whether Mercedes was now considered a possible victim.

"At this time, there is no evidence linking Ms. Colon's disappearance to those of the three girls," the police chief replied. "But we are continuing to look into the situation."

More questions followed, but in the kitchen, Dad and I were no longer paying attention. It felt as if we'd just come out of a trance. The police, the world, everyone would now know beyond a doubt that Dad had had nothing to do with the deaths of those girls. Both of us had tears in our eyes. Had the police arrested someone we didn't know, those tears might have been for happiness. But because we knew Janet/Jane, and because Mercedes was missing, they were only tears of relief. Dad had finally been vindicated . . . at least as far as the murders were concerned. There was still the question of his behavior with the young women, but just for this moment, I decided not to focus on that.

The phone rang. The news on the TV switched to a story about unemployment, and I got up and turned it off while Dad took the call. "Hello?"

I could barely make out a man's voice on the other end.

"Well, I'm both relieved and saddened," Dad began in his "official statement" tone of voice, and I knew he was speaking to someone from the media. "Yes, of course, I'm quite worried about Mercedes Colon. . . ."

A little while later, Dad went outside to make a statement for the news crews, and I went upstairs to see if Whit was online. I felt like talking to him, thanking him, really, for being one of the only people who'd resisted the temptation to rush to judgment about my father.

When I saw that he wasn't online, I thought about calling him, but, remembering that afternoon at the reservoir, I hesitated. I still had the feeling that part of the reason he'd wanted to meet had less to do with Dad than it did with me. Why else would he have been so encouraging about Sarah Lawrence?

That's where my thoughts were when the call came . . . from Whit.

I felt a smile on my lips and realized I was glad to hear from him. "Hi!"

"Good news, huh?"

"Yes . . . I guess, it's just that . . ."

"It was Janet, or maybe I should say Jane. And Mercedes is still missing," he said, finishing the sentence for me.

"It's more than that. I'm still not sure she did it."

"But . . . they've got evidence. The mud and the rope."

"It's just a feeling. You remember how earlier today we were both a little doubtful?"

"Shelby, listen, I was probably wrong about the seriously sick or seriously angry thing. They've got the evidence, and the motive definitely could have been that she killed those girls because they were threatening to go to the police about the scam and she knew she'd get sent back to jail. And that could explain Mercedes's disappearance as well."

I felt a queasy sensation in my stomach. *Please not Mercedes.* "I know that just having a feeling means nothing. Especially when Janet was hiding a criminal past, but it's just such a huge leap from Internet scams to murder."

"But—" he began.

"I have no experience with murderers, so how could I possibly know what I'm talking about, right?"

"Well, more or less, yes."

"What if they *are* wrong, Whit?"

He was quiet for a moment. "You realize what you're saying. If you take the focus off Janet, it goes back on your father."

"Not necessarily."

"Maybe not in *your* mind, but in everyone else's."

"Including yours?"

He paused again, then said, "No. I'm still one of those old-fashioned people who believe that you're innocent until proven guilty. But we both know that's not the way a lot of people in the media world think."

"Well, you're the only one I'm telling this to," I said.

"That's smart. And don't worry, I won't make it the subject of my next story."

I'd forgotten to say that I was speaking off the record. "Thank you, Whit."

"So I'm just curious," he said. "Since you still have this feeling that Janet might be innocent, do you plan to do something about it, or leave it alone?"

"I need to think some more."

"So . . . there's a chance you may decide to do something, even if you don't know what?"

"I don't know. Maybe."

Whit paused again. Rarely has silence sounded more like disapproval. "Do me a favor? Before you do anything, promise you'll talk to me?"

"I promise."

chapter 36

I DIDN'T KNOW what to expect the next day at school. A few people smiled, as if to show that they were happy for me. Others turned and whispered to their friends, just as they had during the first few days of this nightmare. But most didn't react one way or the other, almost as if the story had never existed in the first place.

I was on my way to gym when Ashley Walsh came through the crowd in the hall and blocked my path. "I . . . have to talk to you," she said with a quaver in her voice as she tilted her head toward the girls' room. "In private."

I felt a shiver of unease. What could she possibly want to say? But then I recalled that the last time we'd spoken, I'd had the feeling I'd asked the wrong questions.

Inside the girls' room we primped at the mirror until the bell rang and the other girls cleared out for their classes. If there was one class I knew I could be a little late for, it was gym. As soon as the last girl left, I glanced at Ashley and was shocked to see tears in her eyes.

"What's wrong?" I asked.

"I owe you an apology." She sniffed.

"Why?"

"The reason Tara gives you such a hard time? It's because of me."

It's so strange when you have absolutely no idea what someone is talking about. All I could do was ask "Why?" again.

Her lower lip quivered, and mascara-streaked tears left dark trails down her cheeks. "Because . . . he used me."

I felt my insides go into deep freeze.

"I mean, he . . . he took advantage of me," Ashley said, just to be clear.

I felt a shudder, followed by the most profound feelings of sadness and regret. "Oh God." I put my arms around my old friend while she sobbed and trembled. "You shouldn't be apologizing to me. I should be apologizing to you. I'm so sorry, Ashley. I'm so ashamed. I know what my father's done, but I still can't believe it."

She looked up at me with surprised red eyes. "You know?"

"Not about you until just now, but two days ago, I found out . . . you're not the only one. I don't know how many there were. It's so horrible. I'm so embarrassed to have a father like that." Now I felt my own tears well up and spill out of my eyes. It was bad enough to know he'd done something to girls I didn't know, but to find out he'd done it to someone right here at school—someone I'd been friends with and grown up with—was too much.

Ashley rubbed some tears from her face. "So you understand about the e-mails?"

I took a step back. E-mails? She couldn't mean . . . "Not the ones from vengeance at gmail?"

"Uh-huh."

"How do *you* know about them?" I blurted out.

Ashley averted her eyes and stared down at the floor. "I . . . sent them."

Whatever sympathy I'd been feeling for her instantly vanished. "Are you serious?"

She looked up, a mixture of shame and pleading in her expression. "You understand, don't you?"

"How can you expect me to understand?" I asked incredulously, feeling the blender of my emotions go into reverse, from sympathy to fury.

Ashley stared at me with her red, blotchy eyes. "But you just said—"

I cut her short. "How am I supposed to understand someone who threatens to kill me?"

Her eyes widened, and she frowned sharply. "I never . . ."

"How can you say that?" I asked. "You said I was the last one you'd kill."

She shook her head. "I don't know what you're talking about."

I took out my BlackBerry, scrolled to the e-mail, and showed it to her. "You didn't send this?"

Ashley squinted. "No way."

"It's from vengeance@gmail.com," I said.

She was still staring at the e-mail. "I swear I never sent this."

"You're saying someone else got into your Gmail account and sent it?" I asked doubtfully.

Ashley was still studying the e-mail. "Do you still have the others? The ones I did send?"

"Yes."

"Could you show me one?"

It made no sense, but I scrolled to one of the other e-mails, wondering what fantastic explanation she could come up with. But instead of giving me any kind of explanation, she asked me to go back to the e-mail that threatened murder.

"They're from different accounts," she said. "Look at the address. All of mine are from vengeance one three seven seven three two eight eight. The one threatening to kill you is from vengeance one three seven seven *two three* eight eight. Someone reversed the three and the two."

Now it was my turn to flip back and forth from e-mail to e-mail.

She was right. Not only were the addresses different, but the writing styles, too. Ashley's e-mails were all written in texting style, with abbreviations like "2" for "to" and "U" for "you." The e-mail from the other vengeance wasn't.

Someone else . . . someone pretending to be Ashley . . . had threatened to kill me.

"Oh my God, I am so sorry," I gasped, my jumbled emotions making my eyes grow watery again.

"No, it's okay." Ashley touched my arm. "We all make mistakes. Mine were way worse than yours."

That may have been true, but I still felt miserable and confused. Here was this sweet girl who'd been taken advantage of by my father. The old question gnawed at me: Why? Why would he do something so awful? Were all men like that? Or just my dad? But as painful as that question was, I knew it was less pressing and less immediate than the new question that had formed in my thoughts: if Ashley hadn't sent the e-mail threatening to kill me, then who had?

chapter 37

THE AFTERNOON WAS warm and sunny, one of the last days of Indian summer. When I got home from school, the crowd of media was gone, and Mom was washing her car in the driveway. Her car was something of a family joke because she never drove it farther than the supermarket, and it probably hadn't been outside of Soundview since the day she bought it. And yet, being both frugal and compulsive, once a month she spent an afternoon cleaning and washing it.

"Oh, I can see this car really needs cleaning," I teased.

"Well, it does get dusty," she replied. Maybe it was the warmth of the afternoon, but it seemed like she was in a good mood. The news of Janet being arrested had to be a relief.

"Oh my God!" I gasped playfully. "It's really blue? I always thought it was black."

"Very funny," Mom replied with a smile. "Help me with the mats?"

She'd already washed the floor mats, and they were drying in the sun. We put them back in the car, then she handed me a rag and a spray bottle of Armor All.

"What do you do with it?"

Mom rolled her eyes as if she couldn't believe I didn't know.

"Don't give me that look," I said, pretending to be offended.

"I almost said, 'You are so much your father's daughter,'" she said. "But thank God you're not. Not really."

I knew she'd meant it lightly, but at the mention of his name, things darkened for me, as if the sun had gone behind a cloud. Mom must have noticed.

"Well," she said, as if trying to salvage the situation, "at least they've figured out who did it." She gestured to the bottle of Armor All. "Wipe down the dashboard and interior plastic like the door panels and handles, but try not to get it on the windows."

I did as I was told, and gradually forced the dark thoughts about Dad out of my head. Even though it seemed that I'd been wrong to hope that this crisis might bring Mom and Dad closer, maybe there was still an unexpected silver lining—the crisis might bring Mom and me closer.

She brought the shop vac from the garage and cleaned out the trunk. We worked silently, but I still felt a closeness to her that I'd missed. Once all this was over, I promised myself I would try to patch up our relationship and spend more time with her.

When we were finished, Mom put the car in the garage and we walked back to the house.

For the first time in a very long time, she asked, "How was school today?"

"Not so great."

"How come?"

I hadn't planned on telling her about Ashley, but now I thought that I should. I felt like I needed someone to talk to, and obviously it couldn't be Dad. Besides, Mom already knew about the e-mails from vengeance@gmail.com.

"Remember Ashley Walsh?" I asked.

Mom dipped an eyebrow. "I remember the name. . . ."

"She and I used to be friends, like back when Dad coached my soccer team. She's the one whose father lost his job and they had to sell their house and move into an apartment?"

"Oh yes," Mom now recalled. "Tall and pretty. Sort of quiet."

"That's the one. Anyway, it turns out she was the one sending me those anonymous e-mails."

Mom stopped and stared at me with a quizzical expression.

"She thought Dad was guilty," I explained.

Mom scowled. "Lots of people thought your father was guilty, but they didn't send anonymous e-mails."

Suddenly, I realized that I'd just made a huge mistake. I *never* should have told her. If only I'd taken one more second to think it through, to imagine where it would lead. But now it was too late. She had me. I couldn't even meet her eyes.

"You're not telling me something, Shelby," she said.

"It's nothing, Mom."

"Let me be the judge of that," she said. All the lightness in her mood was gone.

"Mom, please . . ."

"But you'd tell your father if he asked, wouldn't you?"

I felt awful. All those years that I'd taken his side against her without realizing it. All those years of believing him when he said Mom took things too seriously.

"She was one of them, Mom. One of the ones he took advantage of. That's why she sent those e-mails."

Mom's face went blank, and her eyes had that faraway look. The one where it almost seemed as if she wasn't seeing through them.

"Mom?" I said.

She didn't respond.

"Hey, it's been fun doing stuff with you this afternoon," I said. "Why don't we cook dinner together tonight?"

Her eyes darted at me for an instant. She didn't exactly leap at the suggestion, but she did nod. By then, there wasn't a lot of time to prepare the meal, and the best Mom and I could do was make spaghetti and a salad.

"So I'm just curious," Mom said as she chopped some carrots for the salad. "What happened between you and Ashley?"

"I'm not sure. After her dad lost his job and they moved into that apartment, we sort of lost touch."

"Because her father lost his job and they moved?"

"I think it was more than that," I said. "Like she had to spend more time helping her mom at home. And then, from almost the day she turned sixteen, she got a job at Playland. She works really hard. Like every day from one thirty till six and sometimes on the weekends, too."

Mom nodded silently. We'd just finished preparing dinner

when Dad called, sounding grim and rushed. "I have to go down to the police station. Something bad's happened."

I felt myself freeze. "What?"

"Gabe was just found . . . murdered."

FEELING AS IF the floor beneath my feet had just vanished, I grabbed the edge of the sink. "What?" I gasped.

"That's all I know," Dad said. "I have to go." The line went dead.

I closed my phone and stood there, stunned.

"What is it?" Mom asked.

I told her about Gabriel. Mom turned on the TV. A reporter was standing in front of yellow crime scene tape. I recognized the canopy of the building in the background. "Police say a passerby discovered the body behind a Dumpster about two hours ago. It appears that Gabriel Gressen was struck on the head. . . ."

The scene switched to another reporter with Chief Jenkins, who looked even wearier and more beleaguered than the last time he'd been on TV. "We have no reason to believe that this incident is in any way connected with our investigation of the murdered girls."

"Are you saying that because police believe the girls were

asphyxiated, while Gressen was allegedly clubbed to death, it's a different MO?" the reporter asked.

I scowled at Mom.

"Modus operandi," she explained. "Police-speak for the way a criminal behaves."

"I'm saying it because other than the fact that Gressen worked at the modeling agency, there is absolutely no evidence at this time linking these killings," Chief Jenkins replied.

"So you don't believe the serial-killer theory?"

Jenkins shook his head. "We have a suspect in custody for the murders of two of the missing girls. We know that suspect could have nothing to do with this new development. I think that theory was something cooked up by you media people to sensationalize this story."

The reporter ignored the comment. "Do you have any idea why someone would want to kill Gabriel Gressen?"

"Gressen had significant gambling debts, which may or may not have played a part," the police chief answered.

The camera cut to another scene, but I was no longer paying attention.

Gabriel was dead.

Murdered.

Mom turned off the TV and stood at the counter, staring into the backyard. I wondered if she felt the way I did, like things had spun so far out of control that we needed to stop listening in order to make some sense of it.

"What do you think?" I asked.

She shook her head and, without looking at me, said

in a flat voice, "I feel sorry for you, Shelby."

"Why?"

"That you have to be part of this."

Before I could say anything more, a text came in from Roman:
Talk!!!!!!????

I turned to Mom, who seemed to know who it was without being told. She nodded. "Go ahead."

I went upstairs. Roman was waiting for me on the computer. "Can you believe it?" she gasped, sounding nasal.

I shook my head. "No, I really can't."

On the screen, Roman sneezed, then blew her nose.

"You sick?" I asked.

"Not sure. It might just be allergies. But seriously, what do you think's going on?"

"I truly . . . have absolutely . . . no idea."

"The more Chief Jenkins denies that there's a serial killer on the loose, the more I have to wonder," she said, then blew her nose again. Even on the screen, I could see that her nostrils were bright red.

In the silence that followed, my head began to throb, and I realized that I'd been clenching my jaw. Massaging the sides of my head with my fingers, I tried to relax.

"If Janet was in custody, then who killed Gabriel?" Roman asked.

"I have no idea."

"The pool of suspects is shrinking." Roman actually sounded kind of excited.

"This isn't Clue," I reminded her. "We're talking about *real* people. *Real* lives. You and I *knew* Gabriel." Despite what he'd done in the beach-club bathhouse, I took absolutely no pleasure in what had happened to him.

On the screen a chastened Roman pursed her lips. "You're right. Sorry . . . But think about it. Who's left?"

"You mean, who's still alive?" I asked. "Or who's left who could qualify as a suspect?"

Roman sneezed again. "The latter. There's Mercedes. What if she isn't really missing? What if she's just pretending while she goes around killing people?"

"She doesn't drive, so she couldn't have gotten to places like Hartford or Trenton. She isn't strong enough to have taken those girls into the woods, tied them up, and killed them."

"Unless she had help."

That gave me a moment's pause. Whit had suggested the same thing a few days before. There were those tough-looking guys who dropped Mercedes at work each day. "What's her motive?" I asked. "In the history of serial killers, has there ever been a young single mother?"

On the screen, Roman wiped her nose. "I don't even have to look that one up. The answer's no. But that leaves you know who."

I had no idea who she was talking about. "Who?"

"Mr. Amateur Investigative Reporter, who always seems to know everything before anyone else? Pretty amazing for a beginning journalist, if you ask me."

"You're crazy, Roman."

"Can you be *sure*?"

Could I be sure Whit wasn't a serial killer? "He's not

crazy, Romy. He's rational and thoughtful and nice."

"So was Ted Bundy. Handsome, charming, honors student in college, politically active, killed at least thirty young women. Should I continue?"

"No, because then what you're saying is, the night we were in the studio, he arranged to have himself bonked on the head in order to draw the suspicion away from himself?"

"Stranger things have happened. Seriously, Shels? It's not completely impossible."

Was there an iota of possibility in what she was saying? Just because I couldn't imagine Whit's being the killer, did that mean it wasn't conceivable? After all, before yesterday I couldn't have imagined my father preying on young women for sex. Was that part of the problem? That I wasn't a man and therefore couldn't imagine the things men could do?

"Like I said before, Shels," Roman went on, "if it's not him or Mercedes, then who is it?"

It was a good question, but there was one other person who'd been involved from the start. The person who, in fact, had connected two of the missing girls before anyone else, who could have been the one who hit Whit over the head, and who also was always among the first to know the latest news—Roman herself.

AS SOON AS I got off the phone, I called Whit but got his voice mail.

I sat on my bed, trying to think back over everything that had happened since that day the week before when Roman first linked Peggy D'Angelo and Rebecca Parlin to my father. Was there a crucial clue I'd missed? Something so mundane that I'd passed over it without a second thought?

My stomach began to growl, and I realized that not only had I skipped dinner, but I had barely touched my lunch after Ashley proved to me that she hadn't sent the "kill you last" e-mail. As distasteful as the idea of eating felt at that moment, I knew I'd better get something into my stomach.

From what I found in the refrigerator, it was clear that Mom hadn't had much to eat, either. I reheated a small bowl of spaghetti and had just sat down when Dad came in. My emotions were a jumble. If anything, now that I knew that he'd been involved with Ashley, I was angrier than ever at him.

"Any more of that?" He nodded at the plate of spaghetti.

I pointed at the refrigerator.

Dad nuked some spaghetti and poured a glass of tequila. From the way he gobbled down the pasta, it was obvious that he'd also missed a few meals that day.

I didn't want to speak to him, but curiosity overruled my feelings. "Why did the police want to talk to you about Gabriel?"

"They're talking to everyone who knew him," Dad said. "Did I know who he owed money to, or ever hear anyone say they wanted to hurt him? Did I ever see him with anyone who looked suspicious?"

"Did you?"

Dad shook his head. "The only times I saw him outside of work, he was usually with a date."

That brought another question to mind. "Was there one girl in particular?"

"No. I used to kid him that every time I saw him, he had a different piece of eye candy on his arm."

I felt my insides go icy and black. "Not eye candy, Dad. Girls. Human beings. With hopes and dreams and feelings. Not objects."

He bowed his head. "You're right, sweetheart. I'm sorry."

But it was too late. The dam broke. I couldn't keep the anger from spilling out. "Maybe, if you'd understood that from the beginning, you wouldn't have gotten into this mess in the first place."

Staring at the table, he nodded, unwilling, or unable, to look me in the eye. "I've . . . been thinking about that. And . . . I know this won't mean very much. And it won't make up for what I've done. But . . . once I get things under control . . . Or maybe I should say . . . *if* I get things under control . . . I've decided to see a therapist."

It was easy to say, but sadly, I had learned not to count too much on his words. Dad was good at saying whatever he thought was expected without following through. I thought back to Gabriel. "Did the police say what they think happened?"

Dad chewed pensively and swallowed. "They don't know. They really want to believe that it's got something to do with his gambling debts. Because if it doesn't, then maybe Janet isn't the killer after all and they may have arrested the wrong suspect. And that would look really, really bad."

"Did you tell them about him trying to blackmail you?"

"No."

"Why not?"

Dad let the air out of his lungs. "They know he had big gambling debts, so his needing money wouldn't be news."

I stared at him. Once again he was unable to meet my gaze. "But that's not why you didn't tell them, is it?"

He lowered his head. "No, it's not."

I went to bed still trying to make sense of it all, still feeling like the answer was right in front of me and I just wasn't looking at it the right way. In the morning, neither Mom nor Dad was around, and Roman didn't come to school. I assumed her sniffles the night before were from a cold and not from an allergy, but I sent her a text anyway, to find out what she was up to.

After lunch, I was sitting in math when I felt my BlackBerry vibrate. Assuming it was Roman texting back, I waited until class ended before I checked.

The text was from Whit: **Meet @ rez asap!!!!**

I texted back: **Cant. @ schl.**

He wrote: **Lfe/dth.**

Life or death? Was he serious? In any other situation, I would have considered it a gross exaggeration.

But not in *this* situation.

I left school and drove to the reservoir. Whit was waiting in his car. I parked and got out, expecting him to do the same. Instead, I heard his car engine start. He waved for me to get in.

I hesitated. If he wanted to go somewhere else, why had he suggested meeting here? Why couldn't we go in two cars?

He lowered his window. "Come on, get in."

I didn't move. "Why?"

"I need your help with Mercedes."

"What?"

"I'll explain on the way," he said impatiently. "Come on."

Something told me not to. "I don't understand."

"I told you, I'll explain in the car." There was something different about him. Something urgent and tightly wound. I still didn't move. His brow furrowed. "What are you waiting for?"

"Can't we go in two cars?"

He blinked with astonishment. "You . . . don't want to be in the car with me?"

I felt embarrassed and didn't answer. Would he get angry?

Instead, his expression softened. "Oh, man. You really don't know who to trust, do you?"

I nodded, feeling my face flush. Was I being incredibly unfair?

"I understand." His grip tightened on the steering wheel, and he stared straight ahead, as if lost in thought.

"What are you thinking?" I asked.

"How to do it without you."

I GOT IN. Whit started driving.

"What made you change your mind?" he asked.

"You were willing to go without me."

"How do you know I wasn't faking it? Playing you?"

I looked at his profile as he drove. From the side, his bent nose had a bump on the bridge. "Were you?"

He let out a snort.

"So where are we going?" I asked.

"To find her."

"Because you're thinking that if Dad is innocent and Janet couldn't have killed Gabriel because she was in jail, that leaves Mercedes?"

"Yes, but not the way you mean it," he said. "Mercedes didn't disappear. She just wanted to make it look that way. I think she's hiding because she's scared."

"Of?"

"The real killer."

"So you think whoever killed those girls killed Gabriel, too?"

"It's a lot more likely than someone killing him for money."

"Why?"

He glanced at me. "If someone owes you a lot of money and you kill him, will you ever collect?"

He was right. "So you want to find Mercedes and see what she knows?"

He nodded.

"And you need me because you think I'm someone she'll trust," I said. "But what makes you think she'll talk to me?"

He bit his lip. "I hope by the time we find her, you're feeling a little more positive about this."

The "Hispanic" part of Soundview was tiny—just three or four blocks of small houses squeezed tightly together with fenced-in postage-stamp lawns and first-floor windows covered with metal grates.

"What are we looking for?" I asked as Whit drove slowly up one of the blocks.

"Mercedes, or maybe one of her men friends."

Young mothers pushed strollers along the sidewalk. Kids played in the street. Men sat on stoops. "There." I pointed at a low brown car in a driveway. "I think I've seen her come to work in that one."

Whit parked and reached for the door, but I didn't move. "You *sure* about this?" I asked nervously.

He turned and looked at me. "No. Have a better idea?"

For a second, neither of us budged. Then, without a word, we both got out. As I followed Whit up the steps to the house where the brown car was parked, an old man with the stump of a cigarillo in the corner of his mouth curiously lifted his wrinkled face to us. On the porch was a worn, sagging couch; some empty beer cans; and a child's Big Wheel. Whit rang the bell. A moment later the door opened a fraction of an inch, and a woman peeked out apprehensively.

"¿Mercedes *está aquí?*" Whit asked.

The woman shook her head.

Whit launched into Spanish, and they had a short conversation. His command of the language was much better than mine, and he spoke so quickly that I could understand only enough to know that he was pressing her and she was resisting. Finally, she said something about getting her son and backed away, leaving the door slightly open.

A minute passed. A couple of children came to the door and stared at us with big eyes. Then a deep voice from inside growled something, and the kids scattered. A bare-chested, heavily tattooed man appeared. His eyes were puffy from sleep, and his dark hair fell in thick strands into his eyes. He scratched himself and grumbled something in Spanish that sounded like slang. Once again Whit pressed. This time the conversation was even harder to follow. Both of them mentioned Mercedes's name several times. The man kept shaking his head and saying that he didn't know where Mercedes was.

It was obvious Whit didn't believe him. As the tone of the conversation grew tenser, I began to feel scared and was tempted to tug on his sleeve and suggest we leave. But Whit stood his ground. It sounded like he was saying that he was a reporter and was about to run a story about how Mercedes was hiding somewhere here in town and how the police would be very interested in knowing that. And that the only way he wouldn't run the story was if he could speak to her in person.

Finally, the man said that he had to consult someone and closed the door.

"Who's he going to talk to?" I whispered.

"No idea."

The man reappeared with a folded piece of paper and grumbled something threatening about how Whit would be sorry if he didn't keep his word.

The address was a few blocks away, and when we got there, another heavily tattooed man was sitting on the porch, smoking a cigarette. I had a feeling he was waiting for us.

"You from the newspaper?" the man said.

"Yes."

The man glanced at me, then back at Whit. "And her?"

"I'm Mercedes's friend. *Su amiga*," I said.

The man frowned skeptically.

"She works for my father . . . *trabaja para mi padre . . . comprende?*" I explained.

The man nodded, then turned and called loudly inside.

The door was opened by a heavy young woman with long black hair who led us inside to a small den where Pedro was sitting on the floor, playing with blocks. Mercedes was sitting on a couch next to an old woman with white hair. When she saw me, her eyes widened with surprise.

"*Es tu amiga?*" the heavy woman asked.

Mercedes nodded.

"We need to talk with you, Mercedes," I said, and put my hand on Whit's arm. "This is my friend. He's a reporter, and he's trying to figure out who killed those girls. I trust him. I promise he won't tell anyone we saw you. We really need your help. We're not sure Janet is the real killer."

Mercedes stared at her son and didn't reply.

"Janet could go to jail for a murder she didn't commit," Whit said. "That would be a terrible thing. Not just for Janet, but for those of us who believe she's innocent."

Mercedes's eyes were locked on Pedro. He was wearing a blue sweater my mom had knitted for him the winter before.

"Mercedes, we believe you pretended to disappear because you're afraid for yourself and Pedro," I said. "Something is scaring you. If Janet really were the killer, you'd have no reason to hide."

Mercedes blinked. Was she fighting back tears?

"You heard about Gabriel?" Whit asked.

She nodded and a tear rolled down her cheek.

"So you have good reason to be frightened," Whit said.

Except for the sounds of Pedro's blocks knocking against one another, the room went quiet. Even Pedro looked up curiously, as if wondering why the talking had stopped.

Then I thought of something. "Mercedes, there's one other thing I hope you can tell me. It's something I really need to know, because I won't be able to sleep tonight if you don't."

She visibly stiffened, then bent down and gathered Pedro in her arms.

"It wasn't my dad, was it?" I asked. "I mean, I know he did bad things, but please tell me he didn't kill those girls."

Stroking Pedro's head, Mercedes looked up at me with watery eyes. She shook her head and blinked. Tears ran down both of her cheeks. "No, not your father."

I almost missed it. I was so eager to know that he was innocent that I almost didn't get what she was saying. Feeling my jaw muscles tighten, I locked eyes with her and said, "Not . . . *mi padre* . . ."

Mercedes covered her eyes with her hand and turned away. My heart began to thud in my chest, and I suddenly found it hard to breathe. The sides of my head felt like they were in a vice. I looked at my watch. It was a little after one thirty p.m. "We have to go," I said to Whit. "Right now!"

"YOU KNOW HOW to get to Playland?" I asked in the car.

"I think so, why?"

"Just go, as fast as you can."

"Why?"

I couldn't tell him. I couldn't say it out loud. It was only a hunch . . . maybe a strong hunch, but still not the kind of thing I could share with anyone else. I could have been wrong. I *hoped* I was wrong. But there was only one way to know. "Please," I begged. "Just go. Just get us there."

It probably took less than fifteen minutes to get there, but it felt like forever. Playland is an old amusement park with a small Ferris wheel, a wooden roller coaster, and carnival booths where you can try to win a big stuffed animal. On that cool, late October afternoon, the parking lot was nearly empty. We dashed toward the entrance. Of course, like everyone else, we had to pay. Inside the gates, I ran to a target shooting booth where a guy wearing a gray hoodie sat reading a car magazine.

"Do you know where a girl named Ashley Walsh works?" I asked.

He scrunched up his face as if trying to place the name.

"She's tall and thin with dark hair and a red streak," I said urgently.

"Oh yeah." The guy pointed down a row of booths. "She works the octopus."

I sprinted to the octopus, where a short, stocky girl with blonde hair and a stud in her nose was sitting on the fence, looking bored. She glanced up curiously as I rushed toward her with Whit lumbering behind.

"Does Ashley Walsh work here?" I asked, breathing hard.

"Yeah. Why?"

"Where is she?"

"Why do you want to know?" the girl asked suspiciously.

The answer burst out of me. "For God's sake, her life's in danger! Where is she?"

"Are you—"

"I'm *serious!*" I yelled.

I'm not sure which of us was more surprised by my outburst, but the girl straightened up. "She said she was going to go meet someone. She took a break."

"Where?" I asked.

"I don't know."

"How long ago?"

"Maybe ten minutes?"

"Where did she go?" I asked.

The girl pointed at a fence separating the amusement park

from some woods. "There's a hole," she said, "where people go to smoke."

I ran toward the fence and found the gap in the chain link. On the other side were woods and a lake. I squeezed through and turned to watch Whit crouch down and try to follow.

"Come on!" I urged.

"I'm trying," he said. "Whoever made this hole wasn't thinking of people my size. . . . Darn it!"

The back of his shirt was caught, and he couldn't reach behind to free himself. I had to go back and press against him, reaching around to free the material.

I could feel him breathing hard from running. For a moment our eyes met. Then I unhooked the shirt and turned quickly into the woods. The ground under the trees was thick with brush and thorny brambles, but we came to a trail that circled the lake.

"Where are we going?" Whit panted.

"Look for a cave or an opening in the rocks," I said. "Anyplace where someone could hide a body."

"You think the killer's got Ashley?"

"Yes."

"Shouldn't we call for help?"

"There isn't time. . . ."

"We're talking about a killer, Shel—"

I heard a sickening crack and turned just in time to see Whit collapse to the ground in a heap.

chapter 42

BEHIND HIM STOOD my mother clutching a long black metal flashlight. She was facing me, looking right at me, but her eyes had that strange blankness I sometimes saw at home, completely devoid of recognition.

"Mom," I said, my heart racing so fast I felt light-headed.

No reaction. I couldn't tell if she'd even heard me. Whit lay still on the ground between us.

"Mom, where's Ashley?"

Still no response.

"Is she alive, Mom? Tell me you didn't kill her."

Still clutching the flashlight, she stepped over Whit's body toward me, her eyes as empty as a dead fish's.

"Mom? Mom, it's me." I couldn't help thinking how weird it was to hear myself say that. It was stupid. She had to know it was me. The day before, we'd laughed and washed the car and cooked together. "I know why you killed those girls. They were the ones Dad fooled around with, and you felt like they'd ruined everything. You just wanted everything to be nice and perfect for us."

Mom took another step. I didn't know where she was in her mind, but I hoped I could bring her back if I kept talking. "Somehow, you figured out which girls Dad was fooling around with. My guess is you got hold of his password and read his e-mails, right? Part of the information every girl gave in her file was her e-mail and—"

"If it hadn't been for them . . ." Mom said in a flat voice.

She'd heard me. I was starting to get through. "But it wasn't them, it was Dad," I said.

"He couldn't help himself." Her eyes were still dull and her steps almost zombielike.

"You can't really believe that," I said.

She was close now. Her eyes as opaque as marbles. She raised the flashlight. My heart was drumming. "What are you going to do? Kill me, too?"

She didn't answer, just took another step closer.

I was trembling, but I couldn't run away. This had to stop.

Now.

"*Mom!*" I shouted as loud as I could.

She raised the flashlight like a club.

Smack! I slapped her in the face as hard as I could.

She stopped.

And blinked.

The right side of her face turned pink where I'd hit her.

She lowered the flashlight and looked around for a moment as if she wasn't sure where she was.

Then her eyes came back to me, and I saw recognition.

chapter 43

A BREEZE BLEW through the trees, rattling the leaves. Mom and I faced each other. She frowned down at the flashlight in her hand as if she didn't know why it was there, then looked around with a perplexed expression on her face.

"Where's Ashley?" I asked.

She pointed at a gap between some big gray boulders. The opening was just large enough for a person to squeeze through. I hurried to it and called into the dark. "Ashley?"

A desperate muffled sound came out of the inky stillness.

Thank God she was alive!

"It's Shelby. It's okay."

I took the flashlight from Mom and crawled into the gap between the big rocks. Ashley lay in the shadows, gagged, her hands and feet tied. When she saw me, her eyes widened in terror, as if for a moment she didn't know whose side I was on.

"Please," she begged when I undid the gag.

"It's okay," I reassured her. "Nothing bad's going to happen."

Even then she gave me a look like she wasn't sure. As soon as I undid the rope around her hands and feet, she scrambled away through the opening like a terrified animal and then ran. By the time I crawled out, she was fleeing as fast as she could through the woods, back to the fence and Playland on the other side. I couldn't blame her for not wanting to stick around.

Whit was sitting on the trail with his hands on his head. This time, there was blood. Mom stood beside a rock and stared at the water. The whole scene felt surreal. I don't know how I managed to keep it together enough to call the police. Mostly, I think, by trying to make sure Whit was okay. Unlike the last time he got hit, he didn't have much to say. He just sat holding his head and grimacing in pain.

When the police arrived, I told them everything I knew. But when they handcuffed Mom and took her away, I broke down. It was too much. Still, I managed to wait with Whit until the EMS people arrived and put him on a stretcher. The police found Ashley and insisted that she also had to go to the hospital, just to be safe.

They drove me to the police station, where a detective named Payne took my statement. I was numb with disbelief. When we got to the part about Dad and the girls he'd fooled around with, Detective Payne paused and gave me a sympathetic look. "Listen, Shelby, we've been working with the police in Trenton, Scranton, and Hartford. And other cities, too. So we know this part of the story and who some of the girls are. You don't have to go into this if you don't want to."

"I know," I said.

He studied me. "We're pretty sure at least one of those girls was under seventeen. If you're going to tell me what I think you are, I want to warn you that, when a girl is underage, it's considered statutory rape. That's a felony, and in some cases, punishable by time in prison. I just want to make sure that you understand what you're doing by giving this statement."

I understood that Dad would get into serious trouble. He might even go to jail. Even if he didn't, his career as a photographer was probably over.

But then I thought of those girls, and of Ashley, and how he took advantage of them.

I gave the statement.

chapter 44

ON A GRAY morning in November, Roman drove me out to the airport to meet Mom's sister, Beth, who was flying in from China. I was now living with Roman's family and no longer had my Jeep. It had been sold to help pay for Mom's lawyer.

"Thanks for doing this," I said.

"No prob," Roman said. "It's too bad Beth has that flight to Boston in a few hours. We'd be happy to have her come to our house."

Not only had Roman's parents been fantastic about taking me in, but Roman herself had been incredibly supportive about everything. When the story broke and reporters found out that she was my best friend, all sorts of magazines, Web sites, and even TV shows had offered her money to tell what she knew. But she'd refused them all.

At the airport, we waited for Beth to come through security. My temples began to hurt, and I realized I'd been clenching my jaw. I massaged the sides of my head with my fingertips.

"Nervous?" Roman asked.

"You mean, because I'm massaging my head?" I asked.

"You're also tapping your foot a mile a minute."

I hadn't realized I was doing that. "I don't know. It's just . . . so strange. I mean, she's Mom's sister. They've always been really close."

"Shels!" a voice called out. Beth came through the crowd, wearing a bright red scarf. I jumped up and we hugged, and I felt tears rush out of my eyes.

"It's so good to see you," Beth said, holding me tight.

"You, too." Relief radiated through me.

Roman came over, and I introduced them. Beth thanked her for being so kind to me and such a good friend.

"She's worth it," Roman said, squeezing my arm. "So I'm going to go do some window shopping in these fabulous airport stores. How about I come back in an hour?"

She left, and Beth and I sat down in a Starbucks and talked about her flight and teaching in Shanghai and my living with Roman's family and my plans for the future. Beth seemed genuinely glad to see me. Still, it was hard to relax when there was so much we hadn't talked about.

Finally, the inevitable awkward silence came, and it was time.

"I'm so sorry," Beth said.

I nodded. I'd heard those words a lot, and there were plenty of moments when I felt sorry for myself. But it didn't make anything better, and I always tried to get past it.

"There's something I think I should tell you," Beth said. "I think it may help you understand your mom. . . ."

I nodded. In her e-mails, Beth had hinted that there were aspects of Mom's story that I still didn't know.

"You know that she never really got over your brother's death," Beth said. "What you probably don't know is that she always felt responsible for what happened. . . ."

"But he died of pneumonia. . . ."

"She took him outside. It was winter, and she bundled him up and went on one of her hikes. She used to do that with you, too. Put you on her back and walk in the woods for hours."

"And . . . that's how he got pneumonia?"

"It's hard to know," Beth said, "but that's what your mom and dad thought."

"So . . . Mom thought it was her fault?"

Beth nodded. "And so did your dad."

"He . . . blamed her?"

"Yes."

I tried to imagine what that must have been like. Mom blaming herself for the death of her child, and Dad doing nothing to disabuse her of the idea.

"If you want to understand what happened . . . both to your mom and to your parents' marriage," Beth said, "I think that's where you have to start."

"That's why Mom suddenly stopped all the outdoor stuff?" I asked.

Beth nodded. "It was probably too painful for her."

"And Dad fooling around?"

"A way of punishing her?" Beth said with a shrug. "I mean, that's just speculation. We'll never really know. I asked her once why your dad had moved his studio out of the city so suddenly and after so many years."

I stared at her, realizing what the answer would be. "She caught him?"

Beth nodded. "She hoped there'd be less temptation for him in Soundview . . . looks like he proved her wrong."

"But why stay together all this time?" I asked.

Beth's eyes widened slightly. "Because of you," she said, as if it were obvious. "They both love you very much."

"But if Mom loved me, then why would she . . . ," I began, then let the words trail off.

Beth slowly shook her head. "Has anyone ever been able to explain mental illness? Your mom's not the only mother who ever lost a child. And probably not the only one who was blamed for it by her husband. But for her, I guess it must have become too much to cope with."

"But to kill those girls when she herself had a child who'd died . . ."

Beth didn't answer. We watched travelers pass, carrying backpacks and pulling luggage, as if reminding me that even though what had happened in my family had stopped everything, life around us continued.

"I have a question for you," Beth finally said. "What do you think set her off? Your dad moved the studio almost three years ago, but the killings didn't start until last year."

"I've thought about that. I mean, I wonder if for the first

couple of years after Dad moved the studio, she didn't know what was going on? Or maybe she just convinced herself that the problem was fixed? And then something must have happened that . . . you know, made her realize she'd never be able to stop him?"

Beth nodded. "I guess the truth is . . . we'll never really know."

chapter 45

SOMETIMES WHAT SCARES me the most is how close Mom came to getting away with it. She was the one who interviewed office managers and hired Janet. I even have a feeling that somehow she figured out that Janet wasn't who she said she was. Mom planted the mud from the murder scenes in Janet's car and put the rope in her trunk. She sent the e-mail about killing me last because she knew it would throw me off the track. Who would think that her own mother would send an e-mail like that?

She killed Gabriel because she knew if he went to the police about Dad's escapades with young women, we would lose everything, including my chance to go to Sarah Lawrence.

If her mad need for revenge or justice or whatever was going on in her mind had not compelled her to go after Ashley, she might never have been caught. Ashley told the police that Mom had actually begun to kneel on her chest when she heard Whit and me coming and went out to investigate. If we hadn't gotten to them when we did, Ashley might have died, too.

After she was arrested, Mom told the police where to find the third missing girl. She admitted that she'd figured out Dad's passwords and read his e-mails to find out which girls he was fooling around with. The scary thing was, when the police searched her car, they found the files of two more girls she hadn't yet gotten to.

Mercedes had suspected Mom ever since she'd seen her go into the office on several Thursday evenings when she was supposed to be at her book club. Mom must have assumed everyone was gone, but Mercedes had been at the corner waiting for her ride home.

Mom was found to have a severe personality disorder but was deemed able to stand trial. Murder trials take a long time to prepare, and hers only recently ended. As of this writing, she is in prison awaiting sentencing, having been found guilty of second degree murder. I visit her every weekend.

Janet told the police that she was the one who'd hit Whit on the head that night in the studio. Worried that the detectives might discover her real identity, she'd gone back after dark to make sure there was no evidence in the office that might arouse their suspicions.

Dad was found guilty of statutory rape and sentenced to a year of weekends in jail, as well as ordered to enroll for psychological treatment. In addition, more than half a dozen civil suits have been filed against him. He sold the house, the Ferrari, and all his photography equipment, and he still had to file for bankruptcy. He lives in a small apartment and works for an industrial photography company. We have dinner together once a week.

It's now one year later, the fall of my freshman year at

college. Roman's at Skidmore up in Saratoga Springs; I'm living in a dorm on the campus of SUNY Purchase, a state university I'm just able to afford, thanks to scholarship funds and the wonderful and incredible generosity of some people in Soundview.

It's not easy to be the daughter of a murderer, and of a con man who preyed on young women. People naturally assume that there must be something wrong with me, too. It's hard for them to believe that no matter what my parents did outside our home, they still loved and cared for me just like most other parents do for their children. I've given up trying to explain; now I just look forward to the day when I become an ESL teacher. I'd like to teach overseas like Beth, in a place where no one knows who I am or what my parents did.

In the hospital, the doctors discovered that Whit had a linear skull fracture and a concussion, but he's completely healed now. We started dating pretty soon after everything happened. At first I wondered if I was with him only because I felt like I'd lost my family and needed emotional support, but that wasn't why. He's a strong, grounded, wonderful guy, and I'm deeply in love with him.

I guess it should come as no surprise that he's decided not to become a journalist. The public may crave sensational, lurid crime stories, but now that he's seen one up close, he wants no part in reporting on them. Like me, he wants to be a teacher. We may never be able to afford a Ferrari or a fancy house in a place like Soundview, but we'll be doing something good . . . in a world that needs it.

TODD STRASSER is the immensely popular author of *Wish You Were Dead* and *Blood on My Hands*, the first two books of this cyber-thriller trilogy; *The Wave*; *Give a Boy a Gun*; *Boot Camp*; and the hilarious middle-grade Help! I'm Trapped . . . series. You can visit him online at www.toddstrasser.com.

If you enjoyed *Kill You Last*,
you might enjoy Todd Strasser's
other two volumes
of the "thrill-ology":

Wish You Were Dead
Blood on My Hands

EGMONT
We bring stories to life